About

Amaresh Ojha

Founder of India's largest fitness discovery platform, Gympik, Amaresh Ojha is a fitness enthusiast. An IIM Bangalore alumnus, Amaresh has worked with some of the best software companies in the world before setting out to turn his passion into a multi-million-dollar business. A renowned name in the health and fitness industry, his entrepreneurial journey has had an immense impact on his approach to fitness. Originally a native of Bihar, Amaresh now calls Bangalore home.

Subhra Moitra

A writer by day and reader by night, Subhra is a storyteller and fitness enthusiast. Her foray into fitness started as a content developer for Gympik and she has churned out over a thousand articles on various aspects of fitness and wellness. Subhra holds a Master's degree in English literature from RBU, Kolkata.

FITNESS HABITS
Breaking the Barriers to Fitness

AMARESH OJHA
SUBHRA MOITRA

Srishti
PUBLISHERS & DISTRIBUTORS

Srishti Publishers & Distributors
A unit of AJR Publishing LLP
212A, Peacock Lane
Shahpur Jat, New Delhi – 110 049
editorial@srishtipublishers.com

First published by
Srishti Publishers & Distributors in 2021

Copyright © Amaresh Ojha and Subhra Moitra, 2021

10 9 8 7 6 5 4 3 2 1

This is a work of non-fiction, based on the authors' experiences and life-learnings. It provides practical solutions to everyday problems, but the recommendations given herein are in no way intended to be a substitute for professional advice and help.

The authors assert the moral right to be identified as the author of this work.

All rights reserved. No part of this publication may be reproduced, stored in a retrieval system, or transmitted, in any form or by any means, electronic, mechanical, photocopying, recording or otherwise, without the prior written permission of the Publishers.

*This book is dedicated to everyone
who is attempting to make
fitness an integral part
of their lifestyle.*

Acknowledgements

This book has, in essence, been ten years in the making. While the initial learnings and the idea of writing a book were only conceived a few years ago, the work and learning that went into this have been on ever since I started Gympik. My thanks, hence, go first to all the amazing people who have helped build Gympik over the years. It is their hard work and research that have been translated into the learnings in this book. Each one of them is ever in my thoughts and I wish them a healthy and happy life.

My gratitude also goes out to the fitness trainers and coaches who are working behind the scenes and helping millions to improve their lives. They are the true superstars of the fitness industry. Fitness is slowly moving towards an inclusive and holistic experience for many of us because of them.

Thoughts are merely fancy until they are translated into words. I thank my co-author Subhra for distilling my insights into words and dotting the i's and crossing the t's with enormous patience and hard work that built this book. It is no easy task working with the exacting expectations of an entrepreneur. To

Acknowledgements

her credit, she took all the endless reworks and changes in her stride, ensuring that the message of the book shone through.

I thank my wife Kaavya for lending her discerning eye to this project. From the initial editing to the cover designs, she has been an essential part of bringing this book to fruition. Most of all, I thank her for her unflinching support in all my endeavours.

Many thanks to Arup Bose, Stuti and the team at Srishti Publishers for their partnership, support and invaluable inputs along the way. Publishing a book is no simple task, and their insight into the presentation and nitty-gritty of taking a book from concept to the bookshelf has been amazing.

It's no exaggeration that without a legion of people who I met in my life and the ones who are struggling to make fitness a choice are the ones who motivated me to write this book in the first place. They inspired me to share my knowledge in fitness and well-being, and honestly, this book would not even exist had we not crossed paths.

And last but not the least, my thanks go to the readers who are ready to embark on a fitness journey relying on my methods. Thank you for spending your precious time in reading this book.

Introduction

Congratulations! With the simple act of picking up this book, you have reinforced your desire to improve your well-being, hoping to make fitness an integral part of your life. It is an honour to share with you the practices that have helped me go from being a sedentary office-goer to a fitness enthusiast; from hunting for a trainer to building the largest fitness discovery platform in India, thereby helping millions of people find their right fitness choices.

During the initial days of my fitness journey, I was in search of guidance for improving my physique. I looked into all available books and articles on the internet. Most of the available information stressed on zero fat, six-pack abs, size zero, and other fancy jargon. I realized that fitness is still an unknown territory for most people. It was because of the lack of scientifically-backed knowledge and a mind-numbing variety of disciplines that could be followed. As I was new to exercising, these were some of the questions I was constantly struggling with:

Introduction

How do I get started?
What exercise is appropriate for my age?
What do I need to do to fit into that particular dress?
My friends are going to those yoga classes. Should I join them?
Should I take all the advice from trainers at the gym at face value?

I have now been working out for more than a decade. During my time of building Gympik, the largest fitness discovery platform in India, I have interacted with thousands of people and hundreds of trainers in different centres, countries and places. I found that there is no system to certify or accredit trainers or fitness centres on a national level and set some basic checkpoints on the educational excellence of trainers. So basically, anyone who knows some exercises and has been into fitness for some time can become a trainer. It may sound shocking, but that's the reality. This profession is still in its nascent stage as most trainers do not have any formal education to qualify as professional fitness trainers. In India, if you talk to trainers or fitness coaches, they will talk about their training methodology, all of which are different from one another's, and each one of them wants to promote their own ways to fitness.

As an entrepreneur, speaker and fitness enthusiast, I speak at different wellness and startup forums and always

Introduction

talk about the importance of exercise in our life. And every time, I invariably come across the same question: "How do you find time to go to the gym?" I always say that if there's one thing that has the most positive impact on my life, it's a good workout after a tumultuous day at work.

Incredibly enough, though we are aware of the benefits of regular exercising and its impact on our physical and mental health, a lot of us still avoid it. Are we so busy that we do not have time to take care of our health?

Gympik conducted a research on a set of people who had started some form of fitness activity and could not continue. One of the insights was pretty interesting. Close to 20% could not continue for more than two weeks due to various reasons, 40% left between 30 to 60 days, and 20% before 90 days. So overall, 90% of them had dropped out within three months of starting their fitness regime.

Our research included working closely with more than a hundred fitness centres across India. Things that we focused on included enrollment patterns, engagement, renewals and drop practices. According to our findings, out of 100 people who joined a gym, 70 did not renew their membership next year. Some of the top reasons for dropping off, as quoted by those who quit the gym, included lack of motivation, no proper guidance, and not finding time for workouts.

There is an unaddressed gap that needs a fix on the reason behind the increased ratio of drop off.

Introduction

While going through many research studies, I discovered that people tended to quit because fitness did not become a habit for them. This gave us an idea – to look at fitness from the perspective of habit formation, which is well-defined in the book *Power of Habit* by Charles Duhigg.

Our research indicates that it takes at least 90 days for any fitness routine to become a habit, which invalidates the 21-days-habit-formation formula that most of us have been considering to be the ideal habit formation time frame. Fitness is a completely different journey when it comes to habit formation.

Metamorphosing any routine into a habit requires well-timed rewards to keep it going. In this case, the visible changes in the body are the reward for most of us, and that takes time.

The purpose of this book is to establish the fact that fitness is *not* for the few, but for all who want to stay healthy – mentally and physically – and how easily this can be achieved by following simple fitness habit-forming methods. With this book, I will introduce ways to adapt authentic and proven methods from behavioural science to establish a sustainable fitness regimen.

This book stands out from the existing books in the market and the internet about fitness, where the theme shuffles around how to make six-pack abs in thirty days,

Introduction

build muscles in one month, reduce fat in fifteen days, etc. This book is going to be your guide on how to make fitness a part of your life and to continue reaping its benefits for a healthy, happy and contented life.

Fitness, like anything else in our lives, is but a floating mirage, until it becomes embedded in one's daily life. Our decision-making skills about fitness are guided by how we envision fitness. The framework I have shared in this book is an integrated model of fitness and behavioural sciences that will not only guide you step by step and take your fitness game up a notch, but will also work as a prescription on how to make fitness sustainable so that it fits into your lifestyle. I believe this is one of the unique models that stresses on behavioural patterns as well as fitness habit formation that highlights extrinsic and intrinsic catalysts of habit formation.

This book consists of fitness habit-forming action plans based on research data with effective theories. This is especially to help you cross all the hurdles you face in making fitness a habit. The past few years of being an entrepreneur helped me discover ways that are based on proven scientific research on how to make fitness a habit. If you have struggled in the past to put fitness into your busy life, fret no more, because this book can be your ultimate guide to start bringing the fitness factor into your life. That way, you keep receiving the benefits of optimum health and confidence for the rest of your life. This is

Introduction

my attempt to share my knowledge with you to help you make fitness a lifestyle habit, regardless of your age and fitness level.

This book will lead the way for you to make fitness a priority, making minimal but effective changes in your daily routine, formulating a fitness habit, and sticking to it till it becomes your second nature. I have also discussed the norms as well as practices that I think have been followed by the very best to reach their ultimate fitness level. There are certain revelations about fitness and the process through which it can be achieved, which may shatter your long-held beliefs, open a new horizon to look at, and help you understand the concept of fitness and health in a way you have never envisioned till now.

There is no one way to form a habit, but this is the approach that I know has worked over and over again. This book is a compilation of all the tried and tested methods that are effective, regardless of where you stand in your fitness journey. Join me as I take you through a step-by-step guide in approaching fitness, making it a habit, and improving it in the best possible way to build a wholesome foundation for your overall wellbeing.

Amaresh Ojha
GYMPIK

1
Why Exercising Sucks

> *Exercise is like telling your body, "You're gonna hate me for this, but you'll thank me later. The pain you feel today will be the strength you have tomorrow."*

We were sitting in a restaurant, Gaurav and I, on a Friday afternoon. While sipping on mint and lemon infused water, he told me about the depression he had been going through for the past few days after meeting his doctor.

Gaurav Shah, a 29-year-old software engineer, stood five feet nine inches tall, with a 34-inch waist and a chest girth of 40 inches. We have been in touch since the past three years. He is a brilliant software engineer and a fun human being whose four pillars of life – as he told me when we met for the first time at a fitness summit – are coding, cigarettes, chilled

Fitness Habits

beer and music. Originally from Rajasthan, Bangalore had been his home for the past seven years.

Gaurav had called me up the previous week and we decided to catch up for a chat sometime soon. Over the past few years, I have been meeting people from different aspects of life for my book – from techies to football players, entrepreneurs, regular gym-goers and laymen – to understand their health and fitness habits. When Gaurav mentioned having some concerns about his health on the call, I realized that inculcating fitness could make a difference in his lifestyle and overall wellbeing. But, I wanted to hear his side of the story too.

Gaurav turned up at the restaurant with his usual winning smile. I found the burly yet charming guy just as enthusiastic as before, in spite of his depression. The only thing unusual was his increased weight, which made him look older than his age. As he had mentioned earlier, Gaurav had visited the doctor complaining of constant pain on the right side of his lower back. The doctor advised him to take frequent breaks at work, reduce his weight, and maintain a regular workout regime. He also warned Gaurav about the chances of developing acute lower back pain, which is on the rise among people who have regular desk jobs and a sedentary lifestyle. He told me about the depression he

> You should start from where you are and slowly increase your pace.

was going through and his failed attempts at maintaining a regular fitness routine.

"Amaresh, I need some help from you since your advice might just save me from dying early." He laughed.

"Hope everything is fine with you?" I asked, sensing tension in his voice.

"The last few months have been hectic with new product launches, and I feel I am becoming very unhealthy with every passing day," he said.

"You aren't alone. We are workaholics and sometimes we neglect our health so much that it can boomerang on us," I said.

"I am a little on the edge right now. All these health issues came to me as a shock." He managed an uneasy smile while he spoke.

"Are you under any kind of medication right now?" I asked.

"Yes, the doctor has put me on medication for a while. That apart, it looks like my lifestyle needs a change and I have to start exercising to lose the extra weight. It's quite overwhelming for me."

"Why don't you try jogging or walking every day? At least give it a try for a few days?"

"I tried following a few DIY online workouts. Sometimes I tried going for a walk or a jog in the morning. I even started cutting down on junk food and alcohol, and I slashed my calories... but I just couldn't stay motivated to continue all that," he explained sadly.

"What about joining a gym?" I asked.

"Joining a gym isn't an option, honestly. I know nothing about a hardcore workout. Besides, due to extended work hours, I will end up skipping my workouts for sure. I am unable to eat healthy even for a month. I doubt I'll be regular at the gym," admitted Gaurav while nibbling on a French fry.

I wasn't too surprised. I had fully expected him to face these challenges as he was a novice and didn't know how to follow through on his fitness goals.

"I think you should start from where you are and slowly increase your pace. Consider training with a good personal trainer at home or at a gym and maintain a sustainable nutrition plan to bring the change you desire."

"I have never been there, honestly. Besides, I don't know how to find someone reliable, and the nutrition bit is a completely different arena for me."

"I can help you find a trainer you can rely on and can refer someone who can assist you with your nutrition and diet," I reassured him.

Gaurav wasn't sure about his commitment to fitness and told me that he would get back to me for help once he figured out a time to dedicate to fitness. After a couple of months, I checked in on Gaurav. He, like any other beginner would do,

Why Exercising Sucks

started being irregular with his workouts as he couldn't make it a part of his lifestyle. Fitness did not become a habit for him.

Gaurav was forcing himself to work out and sometimes starving himself to get rid of the excess weight. Instead of becoming a way to cure his health issues, fitness had become a punishment for him. He was on the verge of quitting because the fitness goal set by his doctor looked way too far from achievable and reaching there seemed almost impossible to him. He had already given up on the thought of losing 30-35 kgs and decided to quit this constant mental and physical punishment.

Gaurav's case isn't unique! Most of the people around us think of fitness as a miracle pill that will work overnight. They go on a new diet every fortnight, without understanding even the basics of nutrition, thinking it will melt away the fat and help them lose weight. When it doesn't work, they feel frustrated and panicked and fitness starts looking like a struggle. It becomes a never-ending vicious cycle, and they have no clue as to how to go through with it. Ultimately, they quit.

The gap lies in failing to establish a sustainable fitness habit. If you wish to lose weight or get the body you desire, but end up

> If you wish to lose weight or get the body you desire, but end up choosing a path that restricts you too much, it becomes a punishment.

choosing a path that restricts you too much to maintain your normal way of living, it becomes a punishment. When you perceive any activity as punishment, you tend to avoid it as much as possible, just like Gaurav did.

The unfortunate reality is that the impact of fitness is understood by all, followed by some, and embraced by few. Changes, when come drastically, prepare the ground for a major fall. Establishing a sustainable fitness habit that allows you to enjoy your workout time at your own pace, make moderate nutritional changes, and still find food enjoyable, can have a huge impact on your overall health and well-being.

Making smaller shifts in mindset and your way of living can help you develop a lifestyle that you are comfortable with. It helps you develop small shifts with ease. Most of the time, people end up with a one-size-fits-all fitness plan, which seldom contributes to any progress. As a fitness enthusiast and a speaker in the fitness space, I have come to realize that people don't continue with their fitness regime primarily because it *does not become a habit for them; rather, it becomes an emotional struggle that is too restrictive to incorporate as a lifestyle choice.*

Gaurav's story has important implications about how we envision fitness. Children and adults alike find it difficult to bring themselves to the right mindset to make fitness a lifestyle choice. The prospect of physical exertion is terrifying to most people. In this age of instant gratification, the time fitness takes to get results is another deterrent. We expect results too soon. Therefore, the tendency to give up before we can see the positive results puts the final nail in the coffin.

It's not only the stressful experience, but a number of well-established habits – sometimes we refer to them as bad habits or addictions – that obstruct the road to making exercise a habit. It also depends largely on our levels of health awareness and a few parameters that control the choices we make.

Why does physical activity look intimidating?

Ask a fitness enthusiast dripping with sweat about how it feels after a high-intensity workout. You will be surprised to hear them say that it feels euphoric. Sometimes, as they say, that it is a feeling better than sex.

I have spoken to a number of people who run marathons, are into bodybuilding, or follow a regular fitness regime just to stay fit and active. Their answers to the question vary vastly from the answers of people who consider working out as a chore. Sticking to fitness majorly depends on how people visualize it. This impacts the mind and is one of the primary reasons why some people find it easy to exercise and some find it difficult to cope with even the thought of it.

Observing the history of humankind makes it obvious that from prehistoric times, humans had to do a lot of physical activity during the course of their daily lives – to survive in a harsh environment and deal with natural obstacles such as fighting with animals, hunting for food, and surviving against all odds. Even a couple of hundred years ago, people from all segments of society had to go through intensive physical labour to make ends meet – from walking miles to fetch water to procuring food, producing crops to selling them in the farthest market. There wasn't any structured fitness plan dedicated to developing the strength and mobility of early man; rather those were instinctive, necessity-driven practices they had to pursue to survive.

Living in a post-industrial society means that people are habituated to a sedentary lifestyle and the occupational shift from the primeval age to the modern age has decreased their regular physical activities. We are so used to our comfortable and industrialized lifestyle that when we spend our time and energy on any type of activity other than our pre-defined work, entertainment or leisure, we think it is a waste of time.

It's a no brainer that when we only preserve and don't spend, we actually save more. Similarly, when we consume calories more than spending them, we save more and more of them over a period of time. Physical activity, which was earlier a mandate, has now turned into an option. Since a huge amount of energy expenditure is associated with physical activity, we tend to avoid anything that tires us.

Why Exercising Sucks

For most people, fitness is about losing weight or getting a better physique. Looking at fitness as an instant way to achieve short-term goals may backfire and do more harm than good. If you want to work out to lose weight and feel miserable at the thought of working out, you're definitely not going to stay at it for long enough to see results.

Fitness is not always about weight loss. It's about making your body feel better, stronger and healthier. Therefore, fitness is more about a lifelong lifestyle habit than a short-term goal to fix weight issues, build muscle or improve a medical condition. Focusing on building long-term fitness habits that are sustainable can fetch innumerable health benefits that you can be thankful for.

Why do the rewards seem so difficult to achieve?

We like to see quick results when we invest our time and effort in something – be it money, relationships or fitness. And if we don't see the results within the anticipated timeline, we feel discouraged. For a layman, going on a crash diet seems like an easier option to lose weight.

We humans always prefer to repeat behaviours that are immediately rewarding and avoid those that feel like punishment. Fitness falls in the latter category, which often feels

> Fitness is about making your body feel better, stronger and healthier.

like a punishment. When people start a fitness routine, the reward they anticipate is the visual changes in their body. Most people get disheartened when they don't see these changes in a few days.

It's tempting to set extreme goals to lose weight and get a great body. As a matter of fact, the results depend not on your goal, but on the process that precedes it – the repetitions you put in to make fitness a habit. Because being healthy and fit is a lifestyle, not a goal. Often people are trapped in the vicious cycle of following some irregular fitness routine and fad diets to fit into the social standards set for beauty and body structure. But soon it becomes painful, exhausting and wry. They then get demotivated and quit, relapsing into their earlier routine.

Setting unrealistic goals that are too hard to accomplish in a short time make fitness look like an arena for a handful of lucky people. But, if they set a realistic timeline to the same goal, everything changes. Setting achievable targets makes it possible to reap small rewards and helps you stay consistent with your fitness routine. On the other hand, extreme goals that include too much physical exhaustion and dietary restrictions can pull the plug on your fitness journey. It may sound intimidating to set a goal to lose ten kilos in one month and may be eventually disheartening when your body gives up every time you push harder. Rather, setting a goal of losing one kilogram a month by working out for only twenty minutes, five days a week, would sound doable and help you bring consistency into your routine.

Why do we quit the game before it gets interesting?

In the previous pages, I have discussed why we don't like spending energy on things that have no immediate outcome. This psychological trait determines human behavioural patterns and leads to lack of adherence towards any kind of physical activity that causes physical stress or exhaustion, higher heart rate, or exceeds ventilatory threshold (VT)[1]. In fact, the intensity of exercise is one of the major factors why many of us don't like to work out at all.

As each person's metabolism is different, there is no sure formula to predict how soon they will begin to see visible changes in their body after starting an exercise regimen. However, it typically takes several months of regular, dedicated effort before the weight gain or loss is apparent. It is easy to feel disheartened when, after a full month of daily walks or sweat-dripped workout sessions at the gym, you do

---

1. VT or Ventilatory Threshold is the term used to define the point of time and the intensity of any kind of physical activity at which an individual starts experiencing a non-linear way of breathing or ventilation. In simpler terms, during exercise or the kind of exercise that makes an individual breath faster than normal, it is defined as that individual's ventilatory threshold.

Fitness Habits

not hear compliments from your friends on how different you look.

When it comes to maintaining a steady workout schedule, it is way easier to cast off a day's workout for a weekend that calls for a team gathering after a busy day at office. Weighed down by your schedules or seduced by the most sinful pleasures in the world, you decide to make an exception for a day. Many of us may have faced similar incidents – when exercising felt like the least important thing to do. The natural human tendency is to save energy and therefore, it is a big deal to shove off laziness and do what looks like a torturous task.

You have heard it multiple times that to fit working out into your daily life, you need dedication and consistency. But when it is time to take action, everyone gets overwhelmed by one thought – how soon they can get the result. Every change, even if it is the tiniest, comes from a small beginning. It is about taking a decision to make the change and repeating it until the change is ingrained in us. This quote by Danish-American social reformer, photographer and author Jacob August Riis, explains it succinctly:

> The natural human tendency is to save energy and therefore, it is a big deal to shove off laziness.

"When nothing seems to help, I go and look at a stonecutter hammering away at his rock, perhaps a hundred times

without as much as a crack showing in it. Yet at the hundred and first blow, it will split in two, and I know it was not that last blow that did it – but all that had gone before."

We all want the gold but not the grind that is required to dig the gold out. While consistency plays a crucial role in establishing our fitness habit, we often have the question – how can we be consistent with exercising and dedicate our time when we don't even like it? This leads us to the question – why do we not feel motivated enough to make fitness a habit?

Why do we lack motivation?

Before we go about how to make workouts exciting, let me ask – why do you want to exercise?

You may have reasons like – I want to be healthier, want to shed the extra weight, get a better body, want a healthier lifestyle, among many others. The reason behind this undertaking is the cornerstone for your motivation to start fitness. We get that. We all have reasons why we need fitness in our life, we all know how beneficial fitness can be, and we all care about our health and well-being. People who don't follow a fitness routine do care about their health; those who have an unhealthy lifestyle are not doing so to end their lives. We all deeply care about achieving our goals to stay fit and happy.

Fitness Habits

Someone recently diagnosed with type 2 diabetes will start going for a walk, eat healthy and reduce his alcohol intake as advised by the doctor. He will follow all these restrictions and *new* lifestyle hacks to stay away from any further complications his disease might cause. After a week, a fortnight, or a month of following the new lifestyle, he is likely to get back to his favourite former routine as this new lifestyle has too many restrictions and too few immediate apparent results. People are not motivated to adopt a healthy lifestyle even when it is a necessity for survival.

Motivation can be a very powerful, yet tricky affair. Often, getting motivated is very easy and you get caught in a vortex of excitement. Many times, it is almost difficult to find out how to get yourself going and you're stuck in a spiral of procrastination.

You cannot have an incessant supply of motivation in the long run. Motivation is always the outcome of a behaviour. We feel motivated from performing a behaviour, but we often mistake motivation as the reason to start a behaviour. The starting point is a type of active motivation that naturally generates momentum, even in very small ways.

A majority of people fail because they can't decide how to get started. Make the beginning of your fitness so simple and straightforward that when it becomes complicated and demanding, you have the strength to finish it off. You do not

Why Exercising Sucks

need to feel motivated to do the simplest tasks every day, like brushing your teeth or flossing before going to bed. Make it the same with your fitness routine – behaviour that is so easy that you cannot ignore repeating it.

You do not have to be motivated to make fitness a habit. What you need is to omit the need for making a decision every time. An act becomes easier when performed several times, and the excision of decision-making every day is the purpose of a habit. Set a ritual that should be followed at the same time every day to initiate your fitness routine. This eliminates the need to decide; it becomes a ritual that has a pre- and post- action. When your mind is free from the uncertainties of all these questions – What should I do first? When should I exercise? How should I exercise? – you know what your action plan is, and you will automatically follow a fitness routine.

One of the key factors that induces motivation is progress. Motivation can broadly be categorized as extrinsic and intrinsic. Extrinsic motivation is driven by an urge to get external rewards like getting a better body, weight loss, appreciation of others, etc. Intrinsic motivation is inherently rewarding, like the enjoyment of the workout or the feeling of invigoration after a session.

> Motivation can be a very powerful, yet tricky affair.

Fitness Habits

If you are driven by extrinsic motivation, you may be motivated to achieve your fitness goal, but may not always enjoy exercising. The only motivation you might have is to achieve your goal. But what after you have achieved your goal? Are you still motivated to continue your journey? Most often, people who have a fitness goal to accomplish give up once they reach their goal. They not only fail to progress in the long term, but also miss the enjoyment the journey can bestow.

On the other hand, if you are driven by intrinsic motivation, your reason for working out would be simply about enjoying the activity. You continue working out because you love to stay fit, enjoy the workout and how your body responds to it. Even when the outcomes are delayed, you continue following the routine because of the internal pleasure you get from performing that action. Extrinsic motivation in fitness is typically the best influence during the initial stage and can fuel only short-term fitness commitment, whereas intrinsic motivation is the best influence to drive a long-term fitness commitment. If extrinsic motivation influences '*why you **need** to work out*', intrinsic motivation influences '*why you **want** to work out*'.

People who have not developed fitness habits are often driven by extrinsic motivation. They feel a 'need' to work out to achieve certain fitness goals. When you are under the

Why Exercising Sucks

influence of extrinsic motivation, you are going to do what you've got to do, but you're not doing it willingly. External motivation also causes anxiety, and contrary to what we believe, our brain really does not function well under pressure. We tend to lose interest and feel less motivated eventually. Typically, extrinsic motivation works as a driving force to receive the reward almost instantly or in the very near future. For many, fitness is considered a chore and is only performed out of duty. This stands as one of the primary reasons why most people discontinue after or even before achieving their fitness goal.

Whereas people who have already formed a fitness habit are driven by intrinsic motivation – they have adopted fitness as a lifestyle and 'want' to work out to feel the internal satisfaction it gives. Intrinsic motivation drives people to engage in fitness because it is emotionally rewarding – simply working out for one's own pleasure rather than a desire for any external reward.

Essentially, the action (here, a workout of any type) itself is a reward. While exercise motivation involves both intrinsic and extrinsic components, research has shown that extrinsic motivation in fitness is typically the best influence during the initial stage and can fuel only short-term fitness commitment, whereas intrinsic motivation is the best influence to drive long-term fitness commitment.

What is fitness to you?

Different people have different needs when it comes to their fitness regimen. This can lead to a lot of confusion for the novice. One needs to understand what they need and have a basic understanding of the effects of the routines in their chosen form of workout. How much you understand your routine will determine how well you follow it. Seven out of ten people are not sure about which workout works for them and 65% obtain their fitness knowledge from the internet, which leaves them vulnerable to bad or even harmful suggestions, rather than evidence-based guidance when it comes to following the right set of workouts.

There is a lack of trust among beginners about how effective fitness habits can be. A new study reveals that there is a nationwide lack of awareness regarding fitness, which also means that people's tenuous trust in the process interrupts their progress when it comes to committing to fitness. Gympik research finds that 52% beginners do not know how fitness works and 20% of them want to see how their body responds to working out before they decide on continuing their fitness journey.

A 'strategic planning mindset', which focuses on reaching smaller goals, can work as a huge motivating factor. Repeating the routine for reaching smaller goals

> A good workout is a reward in itself.

helps you build the pillars to attain your bigger fitness goals. The more you tick off smaller goals – like improving stamina, strength and flexibility – the easier it is to achieve the bigger picture. This also works as a stepping stone towards continuing with your journey. You feel more confident about your progress and that works as a motivational perk.

Why is it tough to change?

It is human nature to feel empty and discouraged outside of our comfort zone. We are fascinated by the outcome but fail to put in the required effort. Good habits like fitness establish a sense of self-improvement and it is an investment that we make to streamline the best chances life throws at us.

We do not want to accept changes easily, and hence, the effort that is required to make a few behavioural changes in our existing lifestyle seems impossible. Staying in the comfort zone feels prudent, though the opposite is what brings the positive changes in life.

The same is true when we try to fit fitness into our everyday lifestyle. When you have a nine to five job with impending deadlines, it gets difficult to dedicate time to fitness. Hence, committing even ten minutes for fitness might seem like climbing an insurmountable mountain. People fail to stay committed to their fitness routine even when there is an impending health threat.

Fitness Habits

Anything new looks tough in the beginning, and that is why it requires a result-oriented strategy. A change, when it is about stacking fitness habits in your existing lifestyle, does not come naturally. Research shows that planning your actions beforehand – with important factors like 'when' and 'where' to act – increases the possibility of implementation of that action. In the next chapter, we will explore easy yet effective ways to plan actions that will give you desired results.

TAKEAWAYS

- Working out looks and feels hard till it becomes a habit. Once the barrier of the comfort zone is crossed, the fitness habit gets easier to form.
- While extrinsic motivation influences the *'need to work out'*, intrinsic motivation is driven by *'why you **want** to work out'*.
- The chances of continuing a fitness habit increase with achieving smaller goals. Consistency promotes habit formation.
- One size does not fit all! Select a form of workout based on your interest and goals.
- People quit fitness because it does not become a habit for them. Rather, it becomes an emotional struggle that is too restrictive to be incorporated as a lifestyle choice.

2
The Fitness Habit Loop

> *We are what we repeatedly do. Excellence, then, is not an act, but a habit.*
>
> – Aristotle

The root of how habits are formed is embedded in our brain, where a sequence of actions is processed and turned into an automatic routine. Habits develop because the brain is constantly on the lookout for chances to save effort. Regular activities are quickly automated by our brain in order to stop thinking constantly about such basic activities.

William James, an American philosopher and the progenitor of psychology, wrote in his book *Habit*:

"Any sequence of mental action which has been frequently repeated tends to perpetuate itself; so that

The Fitness Habit Loop

we find ourselves automatically prompted to think, feel, or do what we have been before accustomed to think, feel, or do, under like circumstances, without any consciously formed purpose, or anticipation of results."

According to neuroscientists from Massachusetts Institute of Technology (MIT), striatum (a cluster of neurons), which is found in the subcortical basal ganglia of the forebrain is associated with a number of functions, such as motor control, cognitive coordination and emotional functions, and plays an important role in habit formation. The contemporary theory defines a habit as an action or behaviour that needs little conscious awareness to execute in response to a common collection of relevant cues. Research says that approximately 43% of our regular actions are performed almost every day and usually in the same context.

MIT researcher Dr Ann Graybiel – an Institute Professor at MIT and a member of the McGovern Institute for Brain Research – and her team discovered the Habit Loop. This key neurological loop that controls our habits was found more than 30 years ago and this gets a mention in Charles Duhigg's bestselling book, *The Power of Habit*.

In his book, Duhigg carried out an impressive mass of research and relayed interesting facts about habit formation and the ways to break bad habits from the fields of psychology and neuroscience. The book also gives a clear insight into the neurological loop that is the core of every habit – cue, routine and reward.

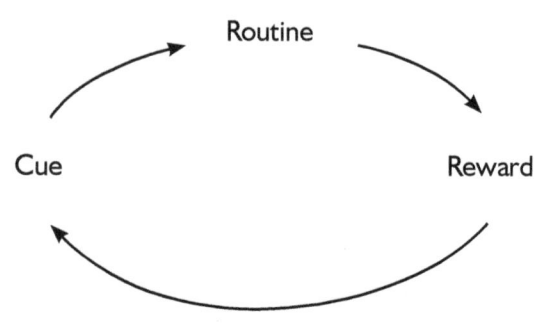

The habit model by Charles Duhigg

As mentioned by Duhigg, a habit loop is a three-part cycle that, with enough time and repetition, converts a certain behaviour into an autopilot activity, and the brain effectively turns it into a habit. Let's see how the three components are related and how the brain responds at the time of forming any habit.

Cue: A cue is the trigger that initiates a behaviour and tells us that conducting that behaviour will get us a reward. Cue can be anything ranging from locations, state of mind, any specific time of the day, companions, physical states, before or after any action, surroundings, sounds, smells, etc. For

The Fitness Habit Loop

example, if you are a smoker, you feel like lighting a cigarette just *after having tea* (cue). Similarly, I feel like going to the gym after *I come back from the office* (cue). The *buzzing notification tone of mobile phones* (cue) leads us to reach out for our phone to check for any notification or message. *The most common and strong cues are time and place.*

Routine: A routine is a habit you perform, which can take the form of an action, emotion or a thought. Prompted by the cue, the routine is the action(s) we take that leads to the rewards we crave for. This could be physical, mental or emotional.

Reward: Reward is the goal of every habit. In neurological terms, a reward is something that constantly reminds the brain to remember the cue and follow the routine so that the anticipated reward is achieved. It is a stimulus that strengthens the entire habit loop and provokes the brain to repeat the routine in the future to get the same reward.

You can actually find out the gateway to master your habits by fixing the first important thing, the *cue*. Once you have mapped out the cue, it becomes easier to follow the same cue that leads you to the routine. This is a powerful strategy because once you have determined the cue, it feels easier

> You can find out the gateway to master your habits by fixing a *cue*.

Fitness Habits

to follow through the habit. Choose a convenient time, place or preceding action to define your cue. Perhaps it's right after breakfast, right after you get up from bed, or it could be when you get home from work. Define your cue, be consistent, and let that be a reminder for you to start your routine. A few examples of the probable cues for a fitness routine are mentioned in the chart below.

MORNING CUES	**EVENING CUES**
You finish your morning rituals	Finish your day at work
After you brush your teeth in the morning	Reach home from office
You have your morning tea/coffee	Thirty minutes before dinner
Your morning alarm rings	7 pm

The prevalent effect of habits in our daily life is a key to understanding the difficulty people frequently experience in changing or modifying their habits. Whether forming a new habit or improving an old one, each habit is made up of a series of actions that lead towards solving a problem.

The Fitness Habit Loop

We often fail in our attempts at changing our habits, since our habits force us to keep doing what we have always done, despite our best intentions to act otherwise.

Various researches have been conducted on rats to figure out the neurological process in the brain. In these studies, researchers found that dopamine is behind creating the desire or the craving for a rewarding experience and pleasure in the brain. The release of the feel-good neurotransmitter dopamine is the answer to why we do what we do. From our basic behaviours like eating junk food, having sex, doing online shopping, spending hours glued to electronic devices, socializing with friends, or dedicating time for our hobbies – each action we perform is associated with the rush of dopamine release in the brain.

The data offers a new insight into this essential neurochemical, which if summarized, stresses the contribution of dopamine in enhancing mood, motivation and concentration, as well as controlling motion, learning and emotional reactions. In follow-up studies, scientists established the fact that the brain experiences a surge in dopamine levels not when the reward is achieved, but when the reward is anticipated. It is the anticipation of rewards that motivates people to act.

When it comes to defining the role of dopamine in habit formation, the crux is that we tend to repeat a habit when it stirs up the anticipation of gratification and satisfaction.

Fitness Habits

The more rewarding and satisfactory the anticipation of the outcome of an action is, the higher are the chances of dopamine spike in the brain.

With the anticipation of reward, there occurs a fundamental shift in the psychological mechanism, and that establishes motivation to act. Rewards work as a motivating magnet, and that, in turn, makes the routine attractive. When we go to a theatre or a musical concert, it is the excitement we feel before the show that causes the surge of dopamine, not after we finish watching it. People who use narcotics or alcohol, feel the spike when they anticipate that it will be rewarding, not after they consume it. Similarly, the anticipation of a rewarding experience makes the dopamine level go up and instigates us to follow the routine.

Scientists discovered that dopamine in the nucleus accumbens, a mesolimbic region of the brain, controls 'wanting' and not 'liking'. Therefore, the concept of motivated behaviour requires more of hedonic impulses and pleasure. In short, 'wanting' denotes the motivational appeal of an outcome that drives us to seek the reward and act to satisfy the craving.

> By anticipating a happy reward in the end, you can stay motivated to work out.

In contrast, 'liking' is the pleasure felt during the consumption of anything with an anticipated reward, whether it is related to food, action, sex or

The Fitness Habit Loop

drugs. 'Liking' is not related to dopamine and depends on very specific brain regions called hedonic hotspots. This explains why, in humans who are becoming drug-tolerant addicts, the motivation to take the drug can grow as they become addicted, so that a single hit of the drug can provoke intense urges to take more, even if the person reports that the dose of drug no longer gives as much pleasure as it initially did.

To understand the power of rewards in creating habits, let us consider how exercise habits emerge. When Gympik conducted research, involving people who have been exercising for more than three months or more, to understand what motivated them to continue working out three to four times a week, the participants said that though sustaining a rigorous exercise was tough initially, with time they learned to cope with the hardship of a workout and craved the reward of feeling good and energized. Continuing for three months or more, they started to crave the feeling of 'accomplishment' post workout.

The sense of self-reward is the biggest drive that pushes you to accomplish and helps you reach a greater height. Countless studies have explained that a cue and a routine are not enough for a habit to stick. People like to stick to any habit when they feel that their hard work is getting paid off, which in turn, creates a sense of gratification. Working out for the initial three months might not show any physical change. However, there is a surge of endorphins and other neurochemicals after a good workout that convinces them that the workout is doing its job.

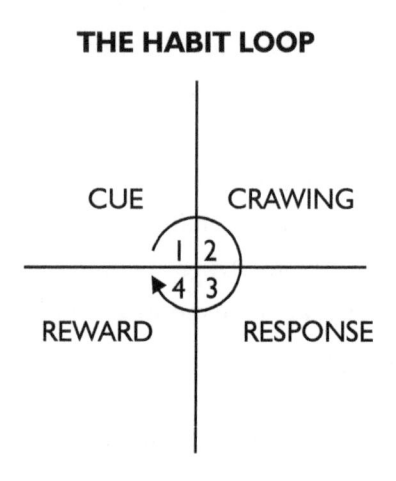

THE HABIT LOOP

```
         |
   CUE   |  CRAWING
     ╱1  | 2╲
    ────────────
     ╲4  | 3╱
  REWARD |  RESPONSE
         |
```

The habit model by James Clear

While Duhigg's habit model defines the three pillars of any habit formation process, James Clear in his bestselling masterpiece on habit formation, *Atomic Habits*, brought up an interesting point. He talks about 'craving', which is the motivation or desire for the reward. Though Clear's habit model is an extension of Duhigg's model, the integration of 'craving', which occurs right after the 'cue', gives Clear's habit model an intriguing tweak. Mere cue, routine and reward are not enough for any habit to persist, unless there is a craving for

The Fitness Habit Loop

the reward. How badly you crave for the reward determines how strong your habit will be. The presence of craving in Clear's habit model makes the habit loop comprehensive. In the next few pages, I will define how each component, especially the *'craving'* of this integrated habit model, is impactful in creating and sticking to your fitness habit.

For someone who wants to lose weight or wants to stay active or get leaner, the thirst for *change* is the key to drive his habit formation. Even when the cue, routine and reward are established, the lack of *craving* for the reward can curtail the habit. Craving makes a habit progressively more automatic, as it creates an urge in the brain to repeatedly seek the same sensation or emotional satisfaction one gets by performing that particular action.

Followed by the cue, craving is the important driving force and the second step of any habit. Without craving, there is no desire to respond or act. It appears in the brain and instigates continuation of the habit loop. It is not the habit we crave, but the shift of an internal state or feeling it delivers.

There is a cascade of habits we follow from the time we wake up till the time we retire to bed. To live, we need habits. Walking, speaking, playing, and reading are all things that first needed our close attention and then a craving is created within for

> The thirst for *change* is the key to drive habit formation.

each habit we have. We crave for morning tea because we are habituated to taking a sip of tea with breakfast. Each of these actions is driven by a craving for the change in feeling or emotion from the current state. We do not crave for a shower, what we crave is the feeling of freshness we get *after* we take a bath.

For example, a colleague of mine joined a gym to lose weight. Losing weight and getting healthier were the *rewards* he anticipated. After work, he would go to the gym, and he practiced this routine for more than 90 days, which is the perfect time period for developing a fitness habit. In spite of that, he quit and could not make the fitness regime a habit. In this scenario, he had his *cue (after work), routine (the workout),* and *reward (losing X kg weight)* defined, then why did this habit fail to ensue?

As mentioned by James Clear in his book *Atomic Habits*, *"If behaviour is insufficient in any of the four stages (cue, craving, response, reward), it will not become a habit."* For my colleague, when the *craving* was insufficient or undetermined, the *desire for change* did not eventuate. Though the cue, routine and reward cycle was followed, a lack of craving for the reward could not let the routine become a habit. Therefore, the motivation to continue with the excruciating workouts depleted over time.

Many people relate exercise to a challenging and exhausting task. One of the greatest challenges we face is when

The Fitness Habit Loop

we encounter a new situation in life or try something new. The initial phase is all about trial and error. Only when this period is over, we seem to have a better understanding of what did not work and how we need to fix a similar situation that occurs at any point of time in life. Something similar happened to an old friend of mine when she started working out without any prior experience of following a workout routine.

The first week was difficult for her; even the following weeks were exhausting, until after a month she decided to quit. After nearly six months, she started her workout again and this time she chose to follow what her friend suggested – working out in groups. She switched to another fitness centre where she would attend mostly group classes with a bunch of twenty people and continued to work out. Even though she had a tough time matching pace with the rest of the members in the class, she loved the energy of working out in a group. Compared to the first time, she was more motivated, which can be interpreted as her developing the *craving* to continue the workout routine.

For her, the first attempt of adapting fitness as a habit failed because the workout routine was not suited to her temperament, and she was not gaining any satisfaction from it. On the contrary, when she started her workout routine the next time, she developed an immediate *craving* to mingle with new people in the class. Associating her fitness routine with a *craving* to socialize changed her mindset towards fitness. And hence, the transition – from seeing her fitness routine as a frightening task to an opportunity to socialize; it kept her motivated until fitness became a habit for her.

These insights reveal the importance of craving in forming a habit. Even when it comes to forming a fitness habit, the dopamine spike is what runs the game. We tend to 'want' what we once liked, i.e. the satisfaction. This leads to the fact that when the liking and wanting are intertwined and of similar values, satisfaction is the outcome. The satisfaction gained from receiving a reward invokes motivational stimuli that prompt us to repeat the same behaviour and form a craving that is essential in forming any habit. The sense of craving for the reward takes us back to the routine that will deliver the reward we experienced before.

While craving for the rewards makes your habit sustainable, time-bound rewards make your habit irresistible. It is worth noting that small progress everyday manifests bigger results in the long run. At the same time, targeting for a time-bound reward keeps you on your toes, your motivation high and your performance progressive. When you make a plan – to run a marathon, to lose five kilos, or save money for your international trip, write a book, or start a new business – you are

> Small progress everyday manifests bigger results in the long run.

The Fitness Habit Loop

making plans for your future self. The only twist here is that you are defining your rewards without defining how soon you want it.

But imagine you want to run a marathon which is going to take place in two months, you want to lose five kilos for your wedding which is three months away from now, you want to save money for your international trip this year-end, you want to write a book before you turn thirty or start a new business next year. In such cases, you are aiming at a time-bound reward that aligns with your craving to get the reward within that time period. When you associate your rewards with a time frame, you reinforce your craving, which amplifies your motivation to attain that specific reward within the given time.

TAKEAWAYS

- The rule that makes the fitness habit stick is – find a *cue*, *crave* for the reward, respond to the *cravings*, and finally, get the *reward*.
- To make fitness a habit, find your fitness cue and stick to it. Make sure the cue is obvious so that the routine is repeated every day.
- Unless there is a *craving* for a reward, there is no desire to bring a change in one's current state of being. How badly you crave for the reward determines how strong your habit will be.

3
The 21-Day Habit-Forming Cycle is a Myth

> *Venturing out of your comfort zone may be dangerous, yet do it anyways, because our ability to grow is directly proportional to an ability to entertain the uncomfortable.*
>
> – Twyla Tharp

Dr Maxwell Maltz was an American cosmetic surgeon and author. In 1950, Dr Maltz started documenting the changes he had been noticing among his patients. He wrote a book that was a compilation of his daily work experiences as a surgeon with profound studies of human psychology. Maltz observed that the expectations his surgical patients often had from their cosmetic surgery were not met until they set a goal of a positive outcome through visualization of that positive outcome. Maltz pursued positive goal setting, self-affirmation and mental visualization techniques in order to help them develop a positive inner and outer goal. This was elaborately defined in his bestselling book published in 1960, one of the psychology masterpieces, *Psycho-Cybernetics*.

In his book, Maltz described that after an operation is done, for example, a plastic surgery of the face or correction of lips or nose, a patient would take at least twenty-one days to get adjusted to the new look. When an arm or a leg is amputated, the patient experiences a phantom limb for about twenty-one days before they adapt to the new situation. Something similar happens when you move to a new house or a new location. It takes approximately three weeks of your stay in that house or the locality before you get adjusted to a place or a new house and call it home.

Maltz's quote, "...it requires a minimum of about 21 days for an old mental image to dissolve and a new one to jell," was misinterpreted since then and used by one and all as a stringent time frame for any habit formation. This is how the 21-day myth was born. Even decades later, the contorted version of Maltz's quote has been extrapolated by self-help book authors, motivational speakers and experts in personal development and coined as 'it takes about 21 days to form a new habit'.

The 21-Day Habit-Forming Cycle is a Myth

The reality: How long does it take to form a new habit?

While writing this book, I had the opportunity to read hundreds, if not thousands, of studies related to fitness habit formation. Among all the research and studies, the one that stands out was conducted by Phillippa Lally, an Economic and Social Research Council postdoctoral research fellow, University College London, and her team. They researched the process of habit formation in everyday life with 96 participants. This study documented experiences of habit development in participants enrolled on a weight loss intervention explicitly based on habit formation principles. They were asked to repeat behaviours of their choice, such as eating a piece of fruit with lunch or doing a 15-minute run every day in the same context for 12 weeks, in response to a cue, and maintain a self-report habit index so as to measure the automaticity of their behaviour on a daily basis.

This research proves that the repetition of behaviour under a consistent environment helps create a link between the cue and the response. Lally and the team found that it took 66 days on average for a behaviour to become automatic. Moreover, habit formation is also dependent on the circumstances, the person and their behaviour pattern. As Lally's research suggests, the truth about forming a

> The repetition of behaviour under a consistent environment helps create a habit.

new habit is – *it takes anywhere from 18 days to 254 days, and not 21 days.*

Though research suggests 66 days as an average number to rely on, it will be unwise to assign any magic number to the habit formation process. Further, the research proposes that while forming simpler eating and drinking habits, skipping a day or two is not detrimental in the long-term; it is those early repetitions that give the greatest boost in making the habit automatic. The data demonstrates that people who were more consistent, were more likely to form the habit.

In 2017, Gympik conducted research to understand the fitness habit-forming pattern among people of various age groups and occupations. This research was carried out in two stages in the form of qualitative and quantitative surveys. In the first stage, in-depth interviews were conducted with individuals of different ages, occupations and marital status. In the second stage, an online survey was conducted across major cities like Delhi, Bangalore, Mumbai and Hyderabad with a total sample size of 1.06 million respondents among the age group of 20-35 years.

On an average, the number of days a person exercises are about three times a week. The research revealed that individuals who participated in at least four physical activity sessions over a twelve-week period are more likely to develop a fitness habit. It takes more than a conditioned cue to carry

The 21-Day Habit-Forming Cycle is a Myth

on with a workout regime, and to make that cue lead to a reward takes a consistent long-term effort.

Gympik's research took into account two separate groups of people – beginners or who wanted to start a fitness routine, and those who have been working out or doing any form of fitness activity regularly or at least four to five days a week for three months and more.

The first group, the beginners, which consisted of 45% of the respondents, reported that they are more likely to continue to work out if it involves some kind of fun activity or causes less exhaustion. Though their goal was to lose weight to improve their health, post-workout exhaustion was one of the biggest reasons that weakened their motivation. About 52% of the respondents found it demotivating to continue when there was no apparent result or visual changes in their bodies.

The second group, the regular fitness maintainers, on the other hand, found it easier to sustain a workout and enjoy it as well. Workout for them had become one of the priorities of everyday life, an automatic behaviour like breathing. People of this group started fitness to reach their rewards and eventually continued even after attaining them. As per the research, the entire process of fitness habit formation took precisely 12 weeks or 90 days.

> Find out what helps you stay motivated and stick to your fitness routine.

Hence, habit formation, in case of fitness, rules out the ideal time of forming a habit, i.e. 66 days, and establishes that *it takes a minimum of 90 days for fitness to become a habit.* Use the workbook given at the end of this chapter to find out how to start doing the groundwork to make fitness a habit.

In this study, the fact that came across somewhat as a boon served as the missing link to habit formation. According to the responses, despite acknowledging fitness as one of the prime concerns to live a healthy life, majority of people do not pay attention to making exercise a long-term habit. Fitness habit formation, when paired with small changes in lifestyle approach, can be identified as behavioural change strategy. Qualitative data of the research indicates that automaticity developed only after the twelfth week and behaviours became similar to the second nature of an individual. Once the habit was formed and started working its way into the brains of the participants, they developed a feeling that enhanced their mood and energy if they exercised. Actions that were initially difficult to stick to became easier to maintain.

The explanation for this is – when we try to follow a routine, the brain values immediate gratification more than long-term benefits. Most of the people who are driven by extrinsic motivation do not get to see stipulated results soon. Fitness needs at least twelve weeks or three months to show

The 21-Day Habit-Forming Cycle is a Myth

any sign of noticeable change in the body. When our brain does not see immediate changes, it feels tiring to continue for months and months to get the reward we anticipate. We tend to lose interest in anything that gets us delayed results. *Similarly, fitness becomes a boring affair and we quit before it becomes a habit.*

Once a habit is formed, the biggest challenge is maintenance. As mentioned above, the average time it takes to make fitness a moderately automatic habit is three months. Forming a fitness habit is difficult; maintaining it is not. The fitness habit-forming theory is that repetitive actions are automatically cued by the environment and thus become easier to repeat when the cue is apparent. This supports fitness maintenance if there are no compensatory changes. Once you have developed a fitness habit, it is easier to practice more flexibility on a daily basis without any fear of losing the normal habitual pattern. Alternatively, beginners need to exercise regularly, maintaining a particular cue, in order to develop fitness habits. But there are hurdles on the way before it becomes a habit that lasts. Rome was not built in a day. Similarly, fitness habits or any habit per se, cannot be built in a day and neither do the results show immediately. You need to cross some critical roadblocks before you reach the phase of excellence.

Sometimes, it is frustrating and makes you give up since there is no visible outcome. But this is because everything

Fitness Habits

looks messy until it is done. A block of iron is of no use until it reaches the melting point. Therefore, if you feel you are not going anywhere, you are not making any progress, or you are struggling – remember that iron melts at a high temperature and you are yet to reach that *melting point* of your habit-forming stage.

To be patient and stay consistent does not mean to give in to laziness. Being consistent is a part of the process, a practice that yields results and helps create sustainable habits. For example, an artistic masterpiece is just a pile of raw materials until it takes its shape step by step with the consistent perseverance of the artist.

Following a regular fitness regime is more like committing to a delayed positive return for an ongoing investment of time, effort and energy. It requires more than just the reward to become a habit. This is precisely why complex habits like fitness demand a *craving* associated with the routine to deliver immediate satisfaction to reinforce the routine the next time. We repeat the routine triggered by a cue only when we are excited about the immediate reward we get from following the routine. In the next few chapters, I will explain how to make your fitness habits progressive, enjoyable and a lifelong reward-bearing routine to follow, even when you slide off track.

> Everything looks messy until it is done.

The 21-Day Habit-Forming Cycle is a Myth

Fitness Habit Workbook 1

Here is a simple exercise to help you introspect and understand your relationship with fitness.

How much do you prioritize your self-care on a scale of 1-5 (5 being the highest and 1 being the lowest)?
1. 2. 3. 4. 5.

1. What do you do to take care of your health?
   _____

2. Do you agree that exercising is a form of self-care?
   Yes   No

3. How healthy are you on a scale of 1-5?
   1. 2. 3. 4. 5.

4. What will be the (simplest) choice of exercise you can do every day?
   _____

5. I like it when I feel _____
   from doing exercise.

6. I do not like it when I feel _____
   from doing exercise.

7. What is your ideal amount of time to spend on exercise?
   _____

8. How long can you spend on your workout?
   – 5 minutes – 10 minutes – 15 minutes – more than 15 minutes

Fitness Habits

9. List down a maximum of two cues that can help you initiate your workout routine:

Morning cues	Evening cues

10. What do you want to achieve from being physically fit?
    - Lose fat
    - Chiseled body
    - Improve medical condition
    - Other [mention _____]

When you are done with the workbook, you have your answer on what you can do to take the first step to make fitness a habit. The bottom line is – you can start your fitness habit by spending at least five minutes every day! In the next few chapters, I will explain why this five-minute routine of your day can prove to be the best investment of your life.

The 21-Day Habit-Forming Cycle is a Myth

TAKEAWAYS

- The 21-day habit formation rule is not applicable when it comes to fitness. It takes at least 90 days or three months to become a moderately automated behaviour.
- Once you have developed a fitness habit, it is easier to maintain the flexibility of your habit without any fear of losing your fitness habit altogether.
- You must establish fitness habits before you try to improve them.

4
Fitness is a Lifestyle to be Lived, not a Goal to be Reached

> *Every good that is worth possessing must be paid for in strokes of daily effort.*
>
> – William James

American neuroscientist David Eagleman said, "Brains are in the business of gathering information and steering behaviour appropriately. It does not matter whether consciousness is involved in decision-making. And most of the time, it's not."

Habits are the brain's internal drivers.

Most people would rather sit and daydream about embarking on a fitness journey than to actually take the first step! It is natural to dream about the end goal, but they forget to plan for and execute the mundane steps to reach that stage.

Fitness is a Lifestyle to be Lived, not a Goal to be Reached

There is a tendency to adopt an all-or-nothing mindset and that is where the fallacy is rooted.

In fitness, going slow or failing occasionally does not mean that there is no progress. The minor changes in stamina and circulation that come with regular exercise contribute significantly to the long-term goals. Accepting this fact and celebrating smaller milestones will help you build momentum and encourage you to stick to your fitness routine. Once the routine is established, forming the habit becomes unforced.

Perhaps the most perplexing of all the questions that remain to be answered is this – *If exercising is so good, why is it so hard to do it?*

The answer to this is a little twisted and requires a longer explanation. It is hidden in the fact that exercise has not been considered as a part of our lives yet. To make it happen, it is important to like what you do and do what you like. It is nearly impossible to master something that you do not like.

If you do not like working out but you want to make it a habit, the effort is similar to a person with a fear of water learning to swim. An activity that is not attractive to you is not easy to learn. Conversely, if you enjoy dancing, the prospect of learning Zumba will be exciting. In an attempt to make fitness a habit, it is pertinent

> If exercising is so good, why is it so hard to do it?

to make it look enticing. This is where *craving* plays the hero.

A workout that feels easy to continue, which is fun or meaningful to you, is a better choice than trying to do high-intensity workouts that make you break out in cold sweat just because you need to get the results sooner. Instead, it is always wise to start with something that is sustainable to perform, and then pick up your pace when your body and mind get habituated to it. The key to effective performance is to know your current limits, put in enough repetitions and refinement to strengthen your competence level, and then expand your limits towards further accomplishments.

Experts often stress on learning the fundamentals first before moving on to complexities of any subject, be it fitness or maths. The first thing you should do to get used to practicing maths is to start with solving easier problems. You start with what you can manage and then, once you gain confidence, go ahead and take it up a notch to solve tougher problems.

In the same way, it is important to overcome the initial hurdle of engaging in exercise regularly and then move the intensity up to the required level. Get it right at a smaller level, get to know what you can control, and know your level of competence before you step up to the next level. This way, there is less chance of you going out of control, sacrificing precision, and failing.

Fitness is a Lifestyle to be Lived, not a Goal to be Reached

In the next few pages, I will unfold the eight pillars of making fitness a habit, and in the following chapters, I will also walk you through all the answers to the questions you have been asking yourself while struggling to make fitness a daily lifestyle choice. I will also guide you on how to implement them in your life by transforming the eight secrets of making fitness a habit into a practical framework that you can use to make fitness your ally. In this framework, I have charted simple rules that you can diligently follow and root out the challenges you are facing in strategizing your fitness habit.

Have you ever wondered and questioned yourself, "Why can I never bring myself to work out to lose that weight?" or "Why is it that I want to get fit but fail to make it consistent?" or "Why does working out never motivate me when I think of getting fitter?"

I'm sure you have asked yourself these questions many times, otherwise you wouldn't have picked this book up. I bet that every time you asked yourself these questions, you were left with no plausible answer.

The answers you are looking for are exactly the answers that lie in understanding the fundamental pillars I am going to propose – *The eight secrets of making fitness a habit.*

If you have ever wondered why you have been struggling to move your body when you actually need to push forward, you will have your answers in the following pages. These secrets will help you discover your current fitness status and guide you to take the next step forward to making fitness a lifestyle choice without fighting against your will.

SECRET – 1

The stepping stone: Awareness

Exercising is a deliberate and reflective process. If you want to build a new habit, you need to be aware of your present state and how crucial it is for you to shift to how much healthier and fitter you want to be. The more you become aware of your current state and your desire for a change, the more you discover something terrifying. You do not have a clue where to start from. The deeper we think, the more we realize that the reason behind our ineffective endeavours is governed by a lack of awareness. Things like working out which you may have never tried before, come with an unknown fear that appears bigger than it actually is.

When you do not know where to start from and how to proceed with your workouts to get the results you want, you are less likely to believe it as a solution to your problem or a means to get benefitted from.

> Things like working out come with an unknown fear that appears bigger than it actually is.

Fitness is a Lifestyle to be Lived, not a Goal to be Reached

The mere thought of excruciating physical exertion clouds the mind and sometimes prevents you from looking forward.

In the process of establishing awareness, we realize that a significant percentage of our feelings, opinions and behaviours are simply manifestations of what we feel at that moment in time. Inevitably, our attention focuses only on issues that already agree with our pre-existing beliefs, even in case of fitness.

A field like fitness, if you have never explored it before, becomes even more difficult to pursue when you do not have a plan chalked out. Whether you are among the ones who may have never done it or someone who has done it in the past but quit, being aware is a powerful tool for you. That is what will lead you to the next step of impactful decision-making.

Even when we know we must make changes in our daily routine; we get overwhelmed too soon and this excitement inevitably fades away before we even reach halfway through. The most effective way I know is to break it down into smaller segments. This way, you will find where you lack focus and pay most of your attention to bridging the gap.

Fitness Habits

Here is a small activity to help you understand your awareness about your fitness level better. Some of the questions may have longer answers, so it is advisable to document all your responses in a journal.

- List your daily tasks – from waking up to hitting the sack _____
- In general, compared to other persons your age, how would you rate your health?
  Poor ☐   Fair ☐   Good ☐
  Very Good ☐   Excellent ☐
- Is the lack of fitness affecting your mental/physical health progress? Yes/ No
- Why do you want to incorporate fitness into your daily routine? _____
- How much time can you spare for fitness every day?
  10 minutes ☐   15 minutes ☐   20 minutes ☐
  more than 20 minutes ☐
- What is it that you do not enjoy about your fitness routine and why? _____
- What will failure in your fitness goal feel like for you? _____
- Tick off the emotions that burden you when you think of fitness:
  - I fear being criticized for my fitness level/my body
  - I fear the exhaustion post-workout/feeling tired/body pain/cramps

Fitness is a Lifestyle to be Lived, not a Goal to be Reached

> - I lack the knowledge in fitness (right postures, right workouts, how long, what suits my condition, what to do next, etc.)
> - I lack clarity (how long will it take to see physical changes)
> - I lack motivation
> - I feel bored doing the same exercises repeatedly
>
> Listing down the answers will help you to acknowledge whether you want to incorporate fitness into your daily life. This is the practice chart to reinforce your awareness of how badly you want to make fitness a habit and this leads you to the rest of the important steps to make fitness a habit.

SECRET – 2

Find your *why*

The famous American author of the bestselling book *How to Win Friends and Influence People* was a lecturer, the developer of self-improvement, salesmanship, corporate training, public speaking and interpersonal skills courses. Dale Carnegie got the idea of writing this book from a short talk. Carnegie was asked to give a short talk on the topic of communication and management. Eventually, the short talk turned into a lecture of one hour and thirty minutes. When the lecture received great response from the masses, Carnegie started getting requests to set up a course around the same subject.

The course became extensively popular and Carnegie was acclaimed by some of his prominent contemporary personalities for his genius contribution to the society. The course integrated all the findings, research, case studies, and thoughts that Carnegie had compiled during his lecture. The success of the course became the talk of the town and an influential subject for having mastery over. This led Carnegie to put all these ideas into a book.

After nearly fifteen years of research, experiments and findings, he wrote the book *How to Win Friends and Influence People*, and since then this masterpiece has served millions of people to ace principles for knowing people better, being a more likeable individual, strengthening relationships, winning over others and influencing behaviour through leadership.

It is remarkable how small actions lead to bigger achievements. Imagine the cumulative effort and time that led to the creation of the book. What started with a short talk became as huge and remarkable as a book.

Discovering your *why* not only guides you through every step you take, but it also helps you progress with a clear vision. The punchline is, your *why* in fitness (let's say, wanting to become

> It is remarkable how small actions lead to bigger achievements.

Fitness is a Lifestyle to be Lived, not a Goal to be Reached

muscular, have a leaner body, lose weight, gain healthy weight, etc.) is a deep-seated purpose that leads you to take the steps on *how* to set your fitness habit and follow through.

Many people do not have their *why* set right. They try to follow fitness without figuring out the fundamental reason as to why they want to make fitness a habit. Unknowingly, we commit to ourselves by saying or thinking, "I will lose weight," or "I will become fitter," without defining why we want to do so. It is crucial to learn to choose intentionally. And to do that, we need to pause to define our 'why' behind it. When we do anything with a clear intention, we are driven by a clear sense of purpose. When you have a clear sense of purpose for why you should work out or why you should bother to make fitness a habit, or why it matters to you – you find a reason to make the change. Without a reason, we have no drive; hence we lack motivation.

When the reasons (*why*) behind your intention to change is vague, it is easier to get caught up in excuses and never being able to bring yourself to the point of doing specific things to get positive results. As I discussed in the second chapter, without craving, there is no action (*routine*). The truth is, the craving lies in defining your *why*. Hundreds of studies have shown that defining the craving serves as an effective tool in sticking to any habit. Researchers further stressed that any habit is formed to satisfy the craving and fitness habit is no different. The greater the craving, the stronger the habit.

Fitness Habits

Here's a small activity to help you define your 'why'.

1. What is your reason behind making fitness a habit?
   Weight loss ☐
   A medical condition ☐
   Stronger and fitter physique ☐
   Leaner body ☐

2. Why do you think fitness is the only option to your goal? _____

3. What do you want to see yourself as by making fitness a lifestyle choice?
   Consistent ☐   Occasional ☐
   Inconsistent ☐

4. How will not reaching your goal negatively impact you on a scale of 1 to 5 (5 being the highest and 1 being the lowest)?
   1 ☐   2 ☐   3 ☐
   4 ☐   5 ☐

5. How will reaching your goal positively impact your health and wellbeing?
   1 ☐   2 ☐   3 ☐
   4 ☐   5 ☐

6. Which areas of your lifestyle need improvement that can be done only through fitness?
   Clean eating ☐
   Better sleep ☐

Fitness is a Lifestyle to be Lived, not a Goal to be Reached

Improved mental health ☐
Better sex life ☐
Better energy ☐

7. What are the rewards (maximum 3) you wish to treat yourself to if you achieve your goal?

_____

The answers you choose will help you find your *why* and how strongly you desire to make a shift from your current situation by making fitness a lifestyle choice. This will also help you understand the perks of making the choice and the drawbacks of not choosing it as a part of your lifestyle.

SECRET – 3

Go slow but go forward

What should your plan look like when you are trying to start something new and do not know how to start? In this case, let's put it this way: What should your plan be when you are starting off a new workout routine or starting afresh when you do not know anything or, rather, know only the basics of fitness? The fundamental truth is to understand that excellence is not compulsory for growth. If you wish to start, 'starting' itself is the more important thing, rather than

Fitness Habits

'mastering' the craft. Bringing yourself to start and slowly pushing yourself to continue is what makes sense when you want to make fitness a habit.

For example, while it might take weeks of mulling over the plan to mend your garden or clean your cluttered wardrobe, once you start the work, it becomes easier to continue and finish the task. Similarly, it takes a great deal of energy to take the first step towards starting your workout. But once you overcome the resistance to getting started, the momentum is set, and it gets easier to carry out the rest of the workout. You cannot finish something that you do not start.

It's the fear of the unknown that cripples the thought of starting fitness. But unless you start going for that jog, doing one push-up, or lifting the lightest weight, you are not making any progress. You can't publish a book that you have not started writing. You can't reach the tenth stair unless you start climbing the first one. Once you start moving, you are bound to reach somewhere farther from where you currently are. So, start with the simplest thing to make a difference – be it a five-minute walk or the simplest yoga move – and make it your daily ritual. Unless you are repeating your actions, you are not getting into the flow of creating fitness as a habit. Therefore, consistency is crucial in forming a fitness habit, even when it means going slow.

> Starting itself is the more important thing.

Fitness is a Lifestyle to be Lived, not a Goal to be Reached

We all expect some rewards from whatever we do and it's no different when it comes to fitness. Rewards drive our fitness habits. But to make fitness a rewarding experience in the long run, you should start as small as you can and stick to your cue every day. Even when you cannot spend five minutes, at least spend two minutes. The willingness to get going is the essence of any journey you choose to accomplish. Typically, the trick to benefit from a workout routine is to find out how little you can do to make it a consistent affair, not how hard you can do it. Simply following the routine, even for a minimum amount of time, helps your brain encode the formation of that habit. You may imagine the process this way – once you perform a certain action at the same time every day, your brain reserves a space for that particular activity at that particular time.

Since exercise is a complex activity, the regular practice gradually eases the difficulties over time and encourages habit formation. If you want to master any habit, you first must consider repeating it. Progress often lies in getting used to the boring process of practicing consistently, sticking to the cue, and making it a routine. Fitness habits are a form of goal-directed automatic behaviour and therefore, consistency in fitness is defined as a ritualistic practice and probably one of the strongest factors in making fitness a habit.

It is true that we plan a perfect goal that looks extravagant and thrilling in the beginning, but it feels like all hell breaks

Fitness Habits

loose when we slacken the pace in maintaining consistency. Most people start missing one workout, which leads to another day off, and when this happens consecutively for more than three to four days, restarting feels like a herculean task that requires double the willpower and motivation. This is when the chain of ritualistic practice breaks, and people quit.

It looks magical from a distance – how someone can run a full marathon or lift hefty weights and make it look effortless. We all wish to be the master, but we fear roadblocks and failure. Mastery is never achieved by chance; it needs consistent practice. Those who have reached there would tell you the story of one simple trajectory they followed – effortful practice, consistently.

The following pages will show you how to master being consistent and how to make practice never sound like a dull affair.

Fitness is a Lifestyle to be Lived, not a Goal to be Reached

Follow this exercise to find how to maintain your 'consistency' in fitness.

I recommend you maintain this sheet as a journal and fill it out every day till you make it an automatic practice to follow this routine.

1. What is the easiest or most fun fitness option for you? _____

2. What is the best time to spend five minutes doing your favourite workout? _____

3. Fill this: After I [do this] _____, I will work out.

4. Fill this: I will work out at [time] _____ at [place] _____.

5. Once I finish my workout, I will reward myself with [reward] _____.

6. After finishing my workout, I feel:
   Amazing ☐   Good ☐   Exhausted ☐
   Miserable ☐

There is a pro-tip that can help you while you are improving your consistency in your workout: *Never miss your workout more than two days at once.*

Record how you feel, track your progress when you wish to increase the time of your workout, and do not break the chain. Even on days when you do not want to work out, just push yourself to do the least, just for the sake of doing it.

SECRET – 4

Add in the fun factor

Our brain is always learning, sometimes without us even thinking about it. Our brain is always choosing good from the bad and deciding to notice relevant cues in each situation, and that is the basis of every habit that we have. We are always influenced by something that we like and avoid things that we do not like. Fitness, in general, has been stitched up with struggle in our mind. Hence, exercising, for a layman, is not synonymous with fun. Interestingly, research suggests that variety in exercise helps people adhere to it by stimulating the brain to fuel the intrinsic motivation towards exercise.

It is easy to get excited about the perfect approach to make fitness work – the fastest way to shed those kilos, the shortcut to become lean or muscular. We are so focused on finding the shortcuts that we ignore the importance of forming a habit in a way that the process itself becomes the source of endless fun.

While fitness requires self-directed action, incorporating variety in the fitness schedule eliminates monotony. Strategies like this work for another reason; it helps increase the intrinsic motivation. It takes time for intrinsic rewards to grow and is very personal. It can only be done through constant trial and error to discover what is intrinsically rewarding about exercise to you. No two individuals are motivated or influenced by the exact same combination of intrinsic rewards to exercise regularly. People find this approach fun and engaging. Various gyms and fitness centres have structured their group classes smartly to make fitness fun and exciting. Different forms of fitness like Zumba, spin class, Pilates, sports-fitness, yoga, HIIT, etc., are designed keeping the mood and tempo of the members in mind. Beginners and seasoned gym-goers will agree that such variations in their fitness regimen increase the percentage of regular and sustained participation.

Nothing sustains motivation better than when you share your fitness habit with a group. It becomes a mutual habit for growth and improvement in fitness. When you attend group classes, you are not worried about losing weight or getting in shape; you are driven by the positive rewards such as mingling with new people, socializing, fun fitness activities, and enjoying the like-minded group vibe.

The more fun and exciting your fitness experience is, the less likely you are to remember it as a drab and agonizing sweat session. We love to look attractive by fitting in the group. If being fit is the desired behaviour of the group, we try to fit in too. When you see a group of people failing and still not giving up, your

> Incorporating variety in the fitness schedule eliminates monotony.

brain tends to conform to the energy. Even when the sessions are hard, it never feels boring. Hence, there is less friction in processing and repeating your fitness routine.

SECRET – 5

Planning before performance
Interestingly, having a plan before you take up a challenge increases the chances of reaching the finishing line – be it preparing your 'to-do' list for your work or your workout. The preparatory phase before starting a workout acts as a cue, helping make fitness a habit. Planning before any workout clears up the mess in the head and will prompt you to follow the routine.

Simply put, planning before performance is considered as a behaviour that accelerates the desire to actually perform the routine. This desire for performing the workout takes place in the brain when we prep the brain to an exercise-ready state. When it comes to forming a habit, exercise has two distinct behavioural phases – a preparatory or planning phase and a performance phase. Each of these phases involves a separate environment with a separate set of actions.

Planning for the workout can consist of various tasks, such as gathering gym materials (water bottle, workout gear,

Fitness is a Lifestyle to be Lived, not a Goal to be Reached

wearing or packing gym clothes) or simply chalking out the kind of workout you are planning for the day. This can mean that the preparation phase could be a part of your morning routine before leaving for work or a routine that you follow before you go for your workout.

Since preparation is not as complex as the performance, establishing a habitual preparation practice could be more feasible than habituating the performance itself. The preparation phase ends as soon as you begin exercising, which marks the commencement of the routine phase. Therefore, the planning for the exercise works as a cue to your workout routine. Whereas motivation stimulates performing the exercise behaviour, the cue of planning functions as a bridge that transfers an individual to the exercise environment. Note down the exercises you want to do on a piece of paper, stick it on your desk, list it in a notepad – do whatever it takes, but ensure you have a plan before you hit the gym.

Our brain is a planning mechanism, and we calculate thousands of pre-planning thoughts throughout the day, anticipating how we are going to do any particular work. It could be simple everyday things like which shirt to choose for work, which task to pick up first from the to-do list, which dish to order from a particular restaurant, or which drink to order. We are constantly planning

> Ensure you have a plan before you hit the gym.

and preparing how to take the next step. Interestingly, the significant effect of planning helps establish habit formation as this builds up the temptation for the routine. The hope that you will be performing your routine the way you plan serves as a reminder and increases the chance of you actually doing it.

Take this test and find out how to pre-plan your workout.

1. How many days a week do you work out?
   2 days ☐   3 days ☐   4 days ☐
2. Do you follow a cue to start your workout?
   Yes ☐   No ☐
3. What time of the day do you prefer to work out?
   Morning at [time] ☐   Evening at [time] ☐
   Late evening at [time] ☐

   Tick off one thing you do just before your workout
   Watch workout videos and create a plan ☐
   Follow a workout plan on any fitness app ☐
   Call your workout buddies who'll join you ☐

Find out which of the pre-behaviours connect with your fitness behaviour. Since no behaviour happens in isolation, figuring out your pre-planning performance triggers your next behaviour. Find out what works for you and stick to the same pre-planning method to make fitness a habit.

Fitness is a Lifestyle to be Lived, not a Goal to be Reached

SECRET – 6

Declutter your cue

You are less likely to miss a cue if you make it obvious by reducing the number of actions you perform at the same time. Which means, keeping the cue decluttered and avoiding mixing up the context of one habit with any other activity. For example, as soon as I return from the office, I eat my pre-workout snack and I am ready to go to the gym. Since reaching home from the office takes place at almost around the same time every day, it reduces the chance of skipping or delaying my pre-workout meal. The simple act of having my pre-workout meal (*cue*) makes it easier to follow the next step, which is to go to the gym (*routine*).

The more obvious your cue is, the lesser are the chances of missing out your routine. The prediction mechanism in our brain is continuously analyzing the information that we are surrounded with. Based on the relevant information, it is constantly helping us to match our decisions with the right information. With constant practice, the cues become prominent and we tend to perform the same task when we notice that particular cue around us. That is the reason why we spend hour after hour scrolling down social

> The more obvious your cue is, the lesser are the chances of missing out your routine.

Fitness Habits

media when we feel bored. We tend to pick up a book and read it when the bookshelf is right in front of us, or we tend to make healthier food choices when we have healthy ingredients in our kitchen.

Additionally, tying your fitness habit with a particular time and place helps you make your habit obvious. The objective is to make the time and place so obvious that when you repeatedly work out at the same place and at the same time every day, you are urged to work out around the same time. When you follow this strategy, you will notice that you start to get fidgety and feel uneasy if you do something else at the time you have dedicated for your workout.

As I mentioned earlier in the book, our preceding action prompts us to carry out the next behaviour. The previous behaviour here works as a reminder and a cue to start our next behaviour. For example, selecting your favorite gym clothes from your closet and placing them on your bed before leaving for work in the morning acts as a reminder for you to go for your workout when you come back home and see the clothes on the bed. This will continue to remain as a cue until you wear them and go for your workout. It evokes a sense of guilt to turn off the cue by placing the clothes in your closet and missing a day of your workout. The purpose is to ensure that the visible presence of the cue becomes associated with no other activities other than your workout. There are many ways to apply such rituals to ensure that you declutter your cue and make it so obvious that it is difficult to ignore.

SECRET – 7

Prep your environment

Your environment plays a critical role in triggering or disrupting your fitness habit. It acts as a subtle cue in itself to trigger our behaviours and shape them into habits. Prepping up your environment can support in forming your fitness habit. I have dedicated a full chapter (Chapter 6) on how environment shapes our behaviour and helps in habit formation, how we mould ourselves according to the environment we are a part of and interestingly, sometimes we pick habits quite effortlessly.

Often, we do not realize how the way in which we design our environment encourages or discourages our habit formation. Consider you want to form a habit of drinking more water every day. The strategy you can employ in making this habit successful is to sprinkle the cues in your surroundings. Place a water bottle on your desk, near your couch where you sit to read, inside your car and other places where you spend time throughout the day. On the contrary, keeping your cue ambiguous (such as going all the way to the water dispenser every time you have to drink water) when you are trying to form 'drinking more water' as a habit will significantly reduce the chances of success. Keeping the positive cues obvious and eliminating distractions help make better decisions easier and increase your chances of responding to the cues.

A comfortable environment that does not stimulate conscious thinking is a perfect ground where your fitness habit can be formed over time. On the contrary, if you do not feel comfortable in a particular environment due to the presence of any negative cues – such as safety concerns, social anxiety, body shaming – then the automaticity process would be interrupted, and you would not be tempted to develop the habit. Therefore, it is obvious that an environment which instigates discomfort or triggers conscious sensory awareness serves as a distraction rather than a cue in fitness habit formation.

Our habit is sometimes defined by our relationship to the people around us. This is indeed a useful way to think about the environmental influence on our habit formation. Our environment is an arena filled with relationships. We tend to maintain and nurture them when they serve us a purpose, in this scenario, helping to form fitness habits. If your workout is associated with a fun environment, with a bunch

> Prepping up your environment can support in forming your fitness habit.

Fitness is a Lifestyle to be Lived, not a Goal to be Reached

of easy-going fellow gym-goers, it feels good to be a part of that group. Over time, your fitness habit becomes associated with the people around you, the fun you have, and the feeling of having had a good time during workout. When the habit you want to form is associated with recreation facilities, you are more likely to perform the routine. It creates a sense of ease and comfort to follow a cue and act on it.

SECRET – 8

Evaluate your progress

The usual restriction of the human mind is to negate the importance of small actions and feel demotivated in the face of delayed results. The mind believes that to achieve something worthwhile, every attempt should be crafted extraordinarily, and steps should be taken accordingly. This, instead of motivating us to start small to go big, holds us back and creates a hollow feeling of fear. That, as a result, fixes our steps in the comfort zone and hinders progress. We are left only *thinking* about taking a step forward, rather than *actually* taking a step forward.

Habit formation is a long-term process. Like I keep stressing, fitness takes at least ninety days to become your habit. And while you wait for the long-term rewards to appear

Fitness Habits

for the time and effort you have put into your fitness habit, you need a boost that keeps you motivated every single day. The brittle truth of life is that the things that matter the most can be achieved only through taking small steps consistently. You will feel more in charge of your fitness habit by breaking down your big goals into smaller ones and evaluating your progress.

Certainly, stopping is not an option when your reward is approaching. From starting with a small jog, home workouts, or spending thirty minutes on any workout at the gym, the idea of evaluating your progress is to limit the number of slips and increase the urge to keep your fitness routine consistent. This process is trusted by many, including elite performers, because tracking improvements are one of the most effective ways to prevent yourself from getting demotivated. It stands as evidence of your hard work and persistence.

Sometimes, it works as a tool to make your fitness habit more addictive. It is easy to fall off the wagon when you feel low or the circumstances are unfavourable, but evaluating your progress serves as a subtle reminder to quickly get back on track so that you do not lose it all. The psychological explanation to this would be that it always feels good to see your growth – be it the money

> Things that matter the most can be achieved only through taking small steps consistently.

Fitness is a Lifestyle to be Lived, not a Goal to be Reached

you invested in the stock market, the raise in your salary slip, or the improvement in your fitness status. When it is tinged with a sense of delight, it is more likely to provide you an immediate intrinsic reward.

While getting in shape and prominent changes in physical appearances can take a little more of your effort, evaluating how flexible you have become, how your stamina has increased, or how your strength has increased over time work as an encouragement mechanism that helps you become more efficient and ultimately serves as an effective tool in forming your fitness habit.

There is always a clump of frustration in the early stages of developing your fitness habit. You expect rapid progress and it's surprising how futile and minuscule these improvements may seem in the first days, weeks and even months. You do not know whether you are even progressing or are totally stuck. This is the reality of the growth process – the most powerful rewards are often delayed. Evaluating your small progresses stand as proofs of your hard work and acts as a subtle reminder to not give up. Improvement is a continuous process that starts with an urge to remaking yourself, every single day.

TAKEAWAYS

- Awareness – When you realize your weakness and work to improve it, it ceases to be a weakness. It becomes a practice towards growth.
- Find your *Why* – Finding out *why* you want to make fitness a habit not only guides you through every step you take, but also helps you move forward with a clear vision.
- Go slow but go forward – Consistency is the key to developing a fitness habit, even if it means going slow.
- Add in the fun factor – If your workout experience is enjoyable and entertaining, it is less likely that you are going to recall it as an excruciating sweat session.
- Planning before performance – The preparatory phase before starting a workout acts as a cue, helping make fitness a habit.
- Declutter your cue – The more obvious your cue is, the lesser are the chances of missing out your fitness routine.
- Prep your environment – We get attached to the environment around us when it works in our favour, thereby helping us to form fitness habits.
- Evaluate your progress – Tracking your progress works as an encouragement mechanism that works as a tool to make your fitness habit more addictive.

5
What Happens to your Body when you Start Exercising Regularly?

> व्यायामात् लभते स्वास्थ्यं दीर्घायुष्यं बलं सुखं।
> आरोग्यं परमं भाग्यं स्वास्थ्यं सर्वार्थ साधनम्।।
>
> **भावार्थ:** व्यायाम से स्वास्थ्य, लम्बी आयु, बल और सुख की प्राप्ति होती है। निरोगी होना परमभाग्य है और स्वास्थ्य से अन्य सभी कार्य सिद्ध होते हैं।
>
> *[The power of regular physical activity has its distinct fan base and the great artists, scholars, writers, thinkers, entrepreneurs and the driven creators of the world have acknowledged and applied it in their lives as a powerful tool to transform the continuous uncertainty, fear of failure, and anxiety into something that fuels the fire of life and turns it into an infinite source of inspiration.]*

Fitness Habits

Haruki Murakami, the most experimental and bestselling Japanese novelist, whose work has been internationally acclaimed and translated into close to fifty languages, wrote a fascinating piece on the similarities between the effort that goes behind running a marathon and creating his extraordinary novels, which are crafted with an immaculate choice of words. In one of his interviews, he mentioned that any creative endeavour or preparing for a marathon is all about practice. Similarly, though talent cannot be acquired, concentration and perseverance are skills which can be improved with training. His book *What I Talk About When I Talk About Running (2008)* reveals the prominent aspect of this great creator's character – his obsession with running and its connection with his creative genius. He said:

"When I'm in writing mode for a novel, I get up at 4:00 a.m. and work for five to six hours. In the afternoon, I run for ten kilometers or swim for fifteen hundred meters (or do both), then I read a bit, and listen to some music. I go to bed at 9:00 p.m. I keep to this routine every day without variation. The repetition itself becomes the important thing; it's a form of mesmerism. I mesmerize myself to reach a deeper state of mind. But to hold to such repetition for so long – six months to a year – requires a good

amount of mental and physical strength. In that sense, writing a long novel is like survival training. Physical strength is as necessary as artistic sensitivity."

This similar thought process is evident to anyone who has been working out for a while or who has incorporated fitness into their lifestyle. There is a wealth of research conducted by neuroscientists that states that exercise is not only about physical health, but it has been discovered that every sweat-inducing workout deeply influences the brain's anatomy, physiology and function, and has an immediate transformative effect.

Exercise and the brain

The brain is involved in everything we do, and it makes us what we are. True that our brain has qualities like intelligence, emotions, decision-making abilities, happiness, strategizing or creativity. The brain stores the greatest power of a man, and when your brain works right, so do you. A healthy brain is the powerhouse of extreme possibilities and yet, we rarely think about giving it the right food, the right exercise to strengthen its power, and unleash its potential to the maximum.

Among many other things – like learning new skills, adequate nutrition, and affectionate relationships –

> A healthy brain is a powerhouse of possibilities.

Fitness Habits

exercise plays a significant role in boosting and enhancing the functionalities of our brains. Distractions, mostly negative, impair our decision-making abilities and drag us towards anxiety, poor eating habits, depression, unhealthy weight gain and whatnot!

There are many outward manifestations that are the result of not considering the importance of keeping your brain healthy. You can see wrinkles on your face or stretch marks on your belly and try your best to do something so that they look better than before. On the contrary, since we can't see the damages we are causing our brain each day by eating unhealthy foods, living a sedentary lifestyle, using drugs or alcohol, or sleeping less, we barely have any idea of how much we are poisoning our brain every day.

Our brain is only about 3 pounds, basically about 2 percent of our entire body weight. It uses 20 to 30% of the calories we consume, 20% of the oxygen we breathe and 25% of the blood flow in our body. A brain tissue is equal to the size of a grain of sand that contains 100,000 neurons and 1 billion synapses, all connected to one another. Information in our brain travels at about 268 miles per hour. We may lose an average of 85,000 brain cells a day if we do not maintain a brain healthy lifestyle. And that makes our brain prone to aging. Science has proved time and again that any form of physical exercise is the fountain of youth and the best medicine for our brains. If you

What Happens to your Body when you Start Exercising Regularly?

want to keep your brain healthy, young and vibrant, move your body every day. Maybe a heavy workout is not your pick on some days. On such days, go for a light walk, a jog, do simple stretching, or easy home workouts. Studies have found that a regular exercise routine helps people opt for better food habits, be more social, reduces the chances of cognitive diseases and insomnia by improving sleep, which is known to have protective effects on the brain. It's a fact backed by studies that performing coordination activities like table tennis, dancing and badminton boost brain activity and keep the brain healthy.

Physical activities improve brain power by increasing action in the cerebellum[2]. Moreover, studies conducted on how aerobic exercises impact our brain functions emphasized on some very important takeaways. Different forms of psychological diseases are the result of lower blood flow to the brain. A good thirty minutes of physical activity boosts serotonin level in the brain, increases blood flow and dopamine in the brain to improve the functionalities of the prefrontal cortex, calms hyperactivity in the limbic system and enhances mood, soothes overactive basal ganglia [3] and reduces the chances of anxiety.

---

2. Containing only 10 percent of the entire brain's volume, the cerebellum carries 50 percent of the brain's neurons.
3. The basal ganglia are situated at the base of the forebrain and top of the midbrain. They are responsible mainly for motor control, as well as other roles such as motor learning, executive functions, emotional behaviours, and play an important role in reward and reinforcement, addictive behaviours and habit formation.

Fitness Habits

While a moderate intensity exercise enhances our brain's health by raising the number of brain cells in the hippocampus region and improves long-lasting memory, it takes just a few daily physical exercises to rapidly increase the mitochondria, the cell power generators. The more mitochondria our cells have, the more energy we get. Hence, working out or doing any strenuous physical activity becomes easier to perform. They are not just the powerhouse of energy; they also strengthen the cells and help in improving overall health and well-being. Moreover, working out not only promotes mitochondrial health, but also stimulates the release of an essential protein called PGC-1 alpha (peroxisome proliferator-activated receptor-gamma coactivator-1 alpha), which helps regulate our metabolism and mitogenesis.

Dr John Ratey, a clinical professor of psychiatry at Harvard Medical School and the author of the bestselling book, *Spark: The Revolutionary New Science of Exercise and the Brain* (2008), mentions that physical fitness has a profound effect on how our brain literally rewires itself.

Any kind of physical activity helps the muscles release FNDC5 (fibronectin type III domain containing protein 5), a protein that blends into the bloodstream and increases the level of BDNF (brain derived neurotrophic factor),

> Physical fitness has a profound effect on how our brain rewires itself.

serotonin, norepinephrine, and dopamine, in the hippocampus area[4] of the brain.

In addition to that, researchers highlight the fact that exercising not only makes us stronger, but also helps in the survival of the fittest mitochondria. Hence, by protecting the fittest mitochondria, regular exercising helps in reducing the chances of developing many neurodegenerative diseases and creating neuroprotective effects in our brain. Meanwhile, physical activity showed clear evidence in causing an improved blood circulation in the overall body and brain. This keeps the brain healthy and also allows more oxygen to be pumped in the rest of our body, helping the mitochondria make energy in lesser time.

Exercise and stress

As an entrepreneur, I hustle a lot between my personal and professional life. I am sometimes talking to investors, keeping employees motivated, working on a critical software release, listening to a nosey client, and so on. Trust me, it is stressful, and I have seen many entrepreneurs smoking a few packets of cigarettes a day to beat it. Alcohol and weed are other stress-busters too, according to many. People find it hard to believe when I say that I have never tried cigarettes and do not consume alcohol very often.

---

4. This area is responsible for learning and memory during physical activity; when it is activated, it promotes neurogenesis.

Fitness Habits

The workout at the end of the day gives me that kick which others may derive from cigarettes and other intoxicants. When I was going through a turbulent phase due to my anxiety issues, the only thing that showed me the way to a healthy life was my workout routine. My attack arrived with no prior warning, but it left a scar, a fear of losing my life. This incident pushed me to look at my health more seriously. I decided to be happy and healthy, rather than sad and unhealthy. For me, my daily workout is something that gives me a sense of accomplishment after a stressful day at work. My way of keeping depression away is to lift weights and, as I tell my friends, I bring out all my stress on the dumbbells and the barbells. A nice and intense workout after a busy day is a divine feeling and a great stress-buster. I have been working out for more than a decade and personally, for me, it's much of a relaxing therapy.

Needless to mention, depression and anxiety are two of the greatest cognitive killers, yet the most ignored forms of disease. Nearly all of us know at least two to five people who have suffered from psychological disorders.

A study by the World Health Organization (WHO) states that at least 6.5% of the Indian population suffers from some form of serious mental disorder.

The National Mental Health Survey, conducted by the National Institute of Mental Health & Neurosciences

(NIMHANS), Bengaluru, reveals that 9.8 million teenagers between the age group 13-17 years suffer from depression or other psychological disorders.

As reported by WHO, 322 million people, amounting to 4.4% of the world's population, suffer from depression. A study conducted in 2017[5] mentions that about 197.3 million people in India had mental disorders, including 45.7 million people with depressive disorders and 44.9 million people with anxiety disorders. The findings also highlight that mental disorders affect one in seven people in India, and the study suggests that between 1990 and 2017, the number of people affected by any form of psychological disorders has almost doubled. Added to that, 20% of Indian mothers are likely to be affected by postpartum depression and 42.5% of corporate employees in India suffer from depression.

The fact that comes into the picture through the various researches in the field of psychology is that depression or stress increases the cortisol level that damages the brain cells, causes memory loss and increases the chances of developing visceral fat. Over the years, psychotherapists have praised exercise as a tool for treating and perhaps preventing cognitive disorders like depression and anxiety. But

> Daily workout gives people a sense of accomplishment and happiness.

---

[5]. The latest data available

Fitness Habits

the effects of physical activity extend beyond the short term. According to Dr Michael Otto, a professor of psychology at Boston University, exercise can also help alleviate long-term depression. It is not only important for treating depression, but also in preventing relapse.

Research also reasoned that daily exercises could help anxious people become less likely to panic. The reason behind this is that during exercise, the body goes through many of the same physical reactions of a panic attack – like heavy perspiration and increased heart rate. Exercising, therefore, is like exposure treatment in several respects. People tend to link the symptoms to safety rather than risk. Psychologists say that a regular exercise routine improves the mood of a depressed individual by helping him return to positive activity and creating a sense of achievement.

There's good data to suggest that active people are less depressed than inactive people. And people who were active previously but quit over time, tend to be more depressed than those who have maintained or started a regular exercise program. Apart from the physical and medical explanations about the positive effects of exercising, there are psychological explanations too.

Exercise, as proved by psychologists, reduces a person's susceptibility to stress. Exercise can be a way to toughen the brain biologically so that stress has less of a core effect, and the impact of exercise in patients with major depressive disorder was usually equivalent to antidepressants.

Psychologists have reported that exercise helps strengthen healthy neural connections in the hippocampus, which is the brain area responsible for verbal memory and learning. A moderate aerobic exercise increases hippocampal volume by 2%, as a result, effectively reversing age-related deterioration in volume by one to two years.

Researcher Schoenfeld and team conducted a study in 2013 that specified how the growth of neurons in the ventral hippocampus gets positively impacted by exercise. The study confirmed that those who exercise, tend to cope with stress better than those who do not.

The hippocampus of an average person who lives a sedentary lifestyle would have underactive neurons that are 'untrained'. These neurons are sensitive and unstable. Moderate to intense physical activity helps promote the development of specific neurons that release GABA neurotransmitters, aka anti-anxiety molecules. These GABA neurotransmitters slow down the firing of other neurons and create a sense of calmness. Scientists agree that exercise soothes chronic depression by increasing serotonin and brain-derived neurotrophic factors that promote neuronal development.

Moreover, daily physical activity helps to regulate blood glucose levels. It benefits people with diabetes and prevents type 2 diabetes. When you work out, your body releases the feel-good neurotransmitters called endorphins. Produced by the central nervous system and the pituitary gland, these endorphins help fight depression by reducing pain and boosting pleasure, which in turn, results in a sense of better well-being.

Exercise and heart health

Moderate to intense physical activity not only delays your aging process by improving and strengthening the mitochondrial life, it has also been noted by numerous scientists that physical exercise plays a crucial role in improving the cardiovascular system in general. Healthcare professionals often recommend engaging in moderate physical activity to help in pumping the heart with more oxygen, transporting oxygen to blood cells and discarding carbon dioxide. It removes metabolic waste products and creates acid balance and hormonal balance in our body. Though the process looks extremely easy, a lot of internal courses of action take place to keep our heart strong and healthy.

First of all, the increase of oxygen in our blood is directly proportional to the amount of blood our heart pumps at the time of our physical exercise. In simple terms, the more our muscles work, the higher the level of oxygen that is thrust into the major arteries

> Daily physical activity helps to regulate blood glucose levels.

What Happens to your Body when you Start Exercising Regularly?

in the body. Exercising helps expand the tiny arteries in the body and transfers more blood to our heart and exercising muscles. The system of the body is smart enough to distribute the blood in different parts of the body by setting a priority. It further optimizes blood flow by reducing the volume sent to the lungs, liver, digestive system and other organs that are not specifically involved in the exercise process directly.

A regular workout routine helps adjust the circulatory system by improving blood flow and increasing cardiorespiratory strength. As a result, our body starts creating more plasma, which, in turn, helps the body to intake nutrients and take away the waste from the system. This entire process works the main pumping chambers of our heart, called the ventricles, which stretch and contract by pumping more blood and flex with greater force. So, if you are one of those who has a history of working out on a regular basis, you may have a bigger and stronger heart muscle than those who do not work out.

As a matter of fact, capillaries – the fine branching blood vessels that form a network between the arterioles and venules – grow in number and transfer more oxygen-rich blood to the muscles. Clearly, an increased number of capillaries also suggest that the left ventricle gets more energy to pump more blood with ease. Hence, if you do moderate intensity exercise regularly, you are less likely to suffer from any kind of heart diseases related to heart muscle damage like arrhythmias, coronary artery disease, etc.

Moderate cardio, or any form of aerobic exercise, protects the heart against dangerous heart rhythm disturbances. Inevitably, the current sedentary lifestyles, poor dietary choices and lack of stress management increase the risk of such diseases even among relatively young people.

Huseyin Naci, an HMS visiting fellow in population medicine at the Harvard Pilgrim Health Care Institute, and a graduate student at the London School of Economics, mentioned in a study conducted on the life-saving benefits of exercise and comparative effectiveness of exercise and drug interventions, "*We were surprised to find that exercise seems to have such powerful life-saving effects for people with serious chronic conditions. Exercise should be considered as a viable alternative to, or alongside, drug therapy.*" Any moderate to high intensity physical activity leads our heart to reach 130-160 beats per minute and pumps up to 20 litres of blood per minute compared to the 5 litres per minute of blood while our body is resting. This and numerous studies have summarized the fact that any kind of physical activity can be as effective as drugs in reducing the risk of death among the average population.

We know that a normal heart beats at 70-80 per minute while we are at rest. The fascinating fact that our heart functions way more differently when we exercise is reflected

What Happens to your Body when you Start Exercising Regularly?

in how it performs when we are more active than usual. It is surprising how our heart reacts to even moderate physical activity, if performed daily. Furthermore, when we are performing any kind of endurance workout like sprinting, brisk walking, playing any sports, running, dancing, swimming or something similar, the heart pumps almost 40 litres of blood, making our heart stronger and more active.

The fascinating reason why an active person has a glowing skin and fitter muscles is that the skin and muscles receive almost 80% of the total blood flow post exercise, whereas, for a normal inactive human being, it is merely 20% of the total blood flow that reaches the muscles and the skin. Maintaining daily physical activity is as good as having medication for life, as it takes care of overall well-being and not just one part of the body per say.

When it comes to building fitness habits, it is always a better option to know what your current state of fitness is. This is one of the best ways to know where you stand now and how to proceed further. No matter how difficult or easy your goal may seem, if you do not know how active you are right now, you will always have a fearful picture about fitness in your mind. Here is a simple way to assess your fitness level and find out your current fitness status.

If you do moderate intensity exercise regularly, you are less likely to suffer from any kind of heart diseases.

Fitness Habits

Take this test to find out how physically active you are.

1. How physically active are you, whether you have a job or stay at home?
   Not active ☐
   I am always on the move ☐
   I am moderately active ☐

2. What is your current level of fitness?
   I am fit and fine ☐
   I am in bad shape right now ☐
   I am kind of okay ☐

3. Do you play any sport/have any hobby like dancing, farming, cycling?
   Nope ☐
   Three to four times a week ☐
   Less than thrice a week ☐

4. Do you help with household chores like mopping, doing repairs, laundry or dishwashing?
   Yes ☐   No ☐

5. Do you take the stairs instead of the lift for climbing two or three floors?
   Always ☐   Sometimes ☐   Never ☐

6. How do you usually get to work?
   Walk ☐   Bicycle ☐   Drive ☐

What Happens to your Body when you Start Exercising Regularly?

Level 2 – Let us take a small practical test
1. How fast can you run in one minute? _____
2. How many push-ups can you do in one minute? _____
3. How many squats can you do in one minute? _____
4. How many jumps can you do in one minute? _____
5. How many steps do you walk daily? _____

I assume you will be true to yourself when you take this self-assessment test. This will help you find your fitness level when you tick off the answers and help you to work on improving your pace.

Exercise and fat burning

Although obesity is obviously a major public health issue, it has proven to be a global epidemic because of its increased prevalence. It has been proved by innumerable studies that as someone's body weight increases, their ability to think clearly and reasonably goes down. This means that if you are overweight and you are not doing anything to reduce the number on the scale, it might be difficult for you, as time goes by, to use your own judgment to become healthy.

Your body is not just a godown for storing extra calories. When you store more calories than your body requires to function, you

> Your body is not just a godown for storing extra calories.

Fitness Habits

send an open invitation to the toxic chemicals that promote inflammation and even damage your brain and overall body function. Therefore, losing weight or keeping your weight in check is not just about vanity, it's a necessity. It is a way to live life without inviting more health hazards.

Although the dangers of obesity have long been recognized, only recently have the advantages of weight loss and exercise become more evident. The effect of weight loss on blood pressure showed that for every 1 kg of weight lost, the blood pressure in the body dropped by 1.1 mmHg systolic/0.9 mmHg diastolic.

Adding to that, reduced weight also helps improve cardiovascular risk factors and improvements in serum cholesterol, low-density lipoprotein cholesterol (also known as bad cholesterol), triglycerides and high-density lipoprotein cholesterol (also called good cholesterol). In simpler terms, excess calories are turned into triglycerides and stored in fat cells in the body. The overall volume of serum cholesterol is the amount of cholesterol in the blood. A high level of serum cholesterol is a problem as it increases the risk of heart disease.

Over the past twenty years, scientists have found in all of us natural molecules that affect our appetite and metabolism, and that is the reason for our weight gain. Why does our body store fat? When we eat more calories than we expend, the excess calories are partially locked up as fat. Our remote

What Happens to your Body when you Start Exercising Regularly?

forefathers did not eat as often as we do. Our ancestors, 40,000 years ago, used to eat a decent meal only a few times a week. The energy they used to get, even when they were not eating, was mostly from the fat stored in the body. Apart from torching fat the right way, helping the body generate more energy and boost overall health, a moderate physical exercise can positively impact our metabolism.

When you perform a range of higher intensity workouts, your body struggles to sustain the intensity, which eventually depletes your muscle energy, and your body consumes more oxygen. A higher oxygen uptake determines a greater level of physiological changes in body fat due to exercise post-oxygen consumption (EPOC). Your exhausted muscles build up lactic acid, which causes that burning feeling, and your body's stores of oxygen become depleted. If you are among those who enjoy a high-intensity workout, you are more likely to work the muscles up and, as a perk, your body works even harder to regain the stores of oxygen.

Several studies and researches affirm that this process of replenishing the oxygen by the body continues for 16 to 24 hours after you are done with your workout. Moreover, the substantial elevation of catecholamines [produced

> A moderate physical exercise can positively impact our metabolism.

Fitness Habits

by the adrenal glands; the catecholamines include dopamine, epinephrine (adrenaline) and norepinephrine (noradrenaline)] is determined by the intensity of the workout you perform. These stress hormones help catalyze your body's fat storage and prepare them to be used as fuel. A high intensity interval training workout can ensure improved VO2 max, i.e. your body's ability to utilize oxygen as a source of energy that also determines building up better energy levels in your body.

Maintaining a regular workout routine is a door to optimum health. In fact, a moderate to high-intensity workout enhances the metabolic machinery in your muscle cells that promotes fat-burning and interrupts fat production. A study conducted by Laval University reveals the fact that high-intensity workouts promote significantly higher amounts of fat oxidation in the muscle fibres, than a lesser intensity steady-paced exercise pattern. Approximately fifteen minutes of high intensity workout performed by a young sedentary male aged between plus or minus twenty-one years reduces the risk of metabolic risk factors and improves insulin functions. Even low volume workouts cause huge improvement in aerobic function of the body. However, the rewarding advantages of performing a daily exercise routine include significant improvements in aerobic metabolism, mitochondrial biogenesis and beta-oxidation.

What Happens to your Body when you Start Exercising Regularly?

Sustaining high-intensity workouts over a prolonged period without running out of breath is challenging for the body. This is because of the way our body uses fuels. During the first 20 seconds of any high intensity workout, our body uses phosphocreatine as a source of energy. Phosphocreatine or creatine phosphate is an endogenous substance present in the skeletal muscle of vertebrates. Phosphocreatine acts as a temporal energy buffer for the first 10-20 seconds of high intensity activity, providing the burst of energy to the muscles. Post 20 seconds, when phosphocreatine depletes, anaerobic glycolysis overrules, and more lactic acid is produced in the body to be used as a source fuel.

Whenever we do any kind of movement, our muscles need fuel to carry out these physical activities and our body mostly uses glucose or fat. When we do any kind of physical activity, be it a brisk walk or any kind of resistance training or weight training, a number of hormones are released from the adrenal glands. These hormones get attached to the specific hormone receptors on adipocytes, which are the cells specialized for the storage of fat. A series of chemical changes occur, signalling the adipocytes that the muscles need fuel to move. Then, adipocytes receive the signals and process the stored fat from the storage to the bloodstream. Once the fat enters the bloodstream, it gets wrapped in chylomicrons so that it can travel to the energy-needing muscles. A sequence of biochemical magic happens upon entering the muscles, and the fat is broken down to its tiniest components, releasing tremendous energy that enables the muscles to move. That is how physical activity puts our muscles at work. These adipose tissues are essentially found throughout our body.

When we do any kind of high intensity workout, our lungs tend to work harder to supply the oxygen. There is an interesting cycle that takes place when we work out; it is like a large number of machines run in the background. This cycle of getting a burst of energy and slowing it down is known as the ATP-PC system.

What is ATP-PC system?

The Adenosine Triphosphate (ATP) stored in muscles breaks down to release energy for muscle contraction. The synthesis leads to the breakdown of ATP to ADP (adenosine diphosphate) and single Pi (phosphate). At the same time, during our workout, the enzyme creatine kinase (CK), or phosphocreatine kinase, or creatine phosphokinase (CPK) breaks down phosphocreatine (PC), which is stored in the muscles, to creatine and single phosphate.

During this process, the energy (Pi + C) released by phosphocreatine results in creating more ATP (ADP + Pi). Now, the newly-formed ATPs are ready to supply more energy to the muscles for high-intensity workouts. Hence, for the initial few minutes of any workout, the body gets the energy from the breakdown of already stored ATP in the muscles, which is followed by the synthesis of phosphocreatine that supplies energy for a few more seconds during the workout.

In a nutshell, the entire ATP-PC system breaks down energy into a few steps for the body to absorb in the easiest form and provides us the energy to sustain the short bursts of intense activity, after which our body requires to replenish the energy. This process needs a couple of minutes, which means, after a bout of intense activity, we slow down and do low or moderate intensity activities before getting back to another intense session. This is the reason why professional fitness instructors allow a rest time of a minute or two after each set of workouts and before starting the next set of intense workouts.

There is an interesting study that talks about how a protein called irisin may help reduce the chances of weight gain. Irisin is an exercise-induced myokine with a peptide structure of 112 amino acids. Researchers have indicated that irisin, this skeletal muscle-secreted myokine, acts as a bridge between exercise and its beneficial health effects, including burning fat, strengthening bones, and protecting against neurodegenerative diseases. There are two types of fat cells in our body – the white fat cells known as white adipose tissue (WAT) and the brown fat cells or brown adipose tissue (BAT). The white fat cells store fat whereas brown fat cells burn fat. Therefore, if you want to lose weight, your brown fat cells should be more in number than your white fat cells. Many recent studies have also found that exercise can increase our brown fat, by generating it or triggering existing cells to burn more fat. The browning of adipose tissue includes irisin. Researchers have discovered that sedentary people generate much less irisin compared to those who exercise.

Irisin is commonly called the 'exercise hormone' because it is released when your cardiorespiratory system is activated, and your muscles are exercised during moderate aerobic endurance exercises. Specifically, the rates of irisin secretion go up as you do more rigorous aerobic interval exercise. Although animal studies are consistent with the link between physical exertion and the release of irisin, the findings from human studies are still a little dubious. Physical activity might even turn some white fat cells into brown.

Making progress is satisfying. The thought of working out becomes satisfactory when we get rewards that are associated with how much effort we are putting into it. Of course, there

> The thought of working out becomes satisfactory when we get rewards.

will be days when you will not feel like working out, there will be days when your body will hurt, and you want to skip that exhausting training. But stepping up and doing it anyway is something you will never regret, I bet. There is no good or bad workout. The only bad workout is the one which is missed.

Coming back to the aerobic and anaerobic exercises, *any high intensity exercise should be combined with moderate and low intensity exercises*. Mixing them up will get you the benefits of both – anaerobic exercises that catalyze fat burn and low or moderate intensity aerobic exercises that improve the overall performance by adding a safe and effective recovery time.

Exercise and aging

How old are you? Before you jump to the quick answer, let me tell you, it's not the one you have been celebrating every year with a progressively increasing number of candles and cake. Know that you have another, even more important age number. I am talking about your fitness age.

Created by researchers from the Norwegian University of Science and Technology, your fitness age takes your respiratory health into account and is made up of different components including your heart rate, waist circumference, exercise routine and many other parametres.

You can go ahead and calculate your fitness age here https://www.amareshojha.com/fitness-age.

If you are wondering why you should even care about the number that pops up on your screen, let me tell you why knowing your fitness age can take you a long way. According to researchers from the above university, your fitness age is the deciding factor in your life expectancy. The lower your fitness age is from your actual age, the higher your chances are of living a longer and healthier life. After plugging in your stats, if the results show a higher number, you might have to up your fitness game. Over a period of time, if you stay committed to a regular fitness routine, it will help you decrease your fitness age.

> Muscle mitochondrial dysfunction is apparent with age. Starting from decrease in mitochondrial DNA copy number, muscle mitochondrial function changes include many alterations in the mitochondria that include reduced muscle mitochondrial oxidative enzyme functions, decreased messenger RNA (mRNA) concentrations in genes encoding muscle mitochondrial proteins, and less active mitochondrial protein synthesis. Physical activity helps break down the muscle mitochondrial adenosine triphosphate (ATP) that is stored in muscles, which breaks down to release energy for muscle contraction. High

intensity interval workouts enhance the mitochondrial function and protein synthesis in the muscles, which help increase muscle hypertrophy and stave off the age-related internal deterioration.

However, the synthesis leads to the breakdown of ATP to ADP and single Pi. At the same time, during workouts, the enzyme creatine kinase, or phosphocreatine kinase, or creatine phosphokinase breaks down phosphocreatine, which is stored in the muscles, to creatine and single phosphate. During this process, the energy (Pi + C) released by phosphocreatine results in creating more ATP (ADP + Pi). Now, the newly-formed ATPs are ready to supply more energy to the muscles for high intensity workouts.

With age, the structural changes and the reduction in the mitochondrial ATP production could also be the reason for increased muscle weakness. A number of research studies and evidence suggest that an increased oxidative damage to mitochondrial DNA (mtDNA) with aging and accumulated damage to DNA may explain an overall reduction in mtDNA copy numbers in oxidative tissue, such as skeletal muscle. Reduced mtDNA copy number can lead to a reduction in MessengerRNA (mRNA) abundance, resulting in reduced mitochondrial protein synthesis and activity of the enzymes. A large amount of evidence indicates oxidative damage to mtDNA as a determinant event occurring during aging that can cause or increase mitochondrial dysfunction, thereby causing neurodegenerative events.

When diabetes researcher at the Mayo Clinic in Rochester, Minnesota, Dr Sreekumaran Nair and his team conducted research on how exercise helps in staving off age, they discovered something interesting. They found that high intensity interval training can be remarkably beneficial, not only aiding in weight loss but also in obtaining the greatest cellular gain. The reason behind its incredible results on fat burning is that it shoots up your metabolism when the workouts are structured into a tension styled program. If you follow a high intensity interval workout, it enhances the mitochondrial function and protein synthesis in the muscles, resulting in increased muscle hypertrophy, which in turn staves off age-related internal deterioration.

Exercise and bones

Bones are living, active tissues that are constantly being remodelled by the continuous building and dismantling process.

Our body builds bone faster early in our life. But with age, bones become more brittle and vulnerable to breakage. Exercising, as a matter of fact, contributes to improved bone structure, strength and density by the pulling, pressing, and twisting of muscles caused by the physical activity. Exercising, especially resistance exercise, helps in developing an optimal bone architecture and high bone strength. Like muscle, bone is living tissue that responds to exercise that put pressure on the bones, and help activate the bone cells to make them stronger. A person who maintains a regular exercise routine have maximum bone density and strength than those who do not. For most, during the third decade of life is the time when we begin to lose bone. Exercise is known to be a mind-body-soul coordination that not only helps preserve muscle strength, but also develops balance and proper posture. This, in turn, helps to prevent falls and related fractures as we age.

A regular fitness routine will help bones retain strength that may otherwise be lost due to changes related to age and hormones. Evidence says, a high degree of physical activity during childhood has a beneficial impact on bone mass and helps to reduce bone loss due to aging. Moreover, aerobic exercise is known to stimulate preferentially mitochondrial biogenesis and protein synthesis involved in oxidative phosphorylation, while resistance exercise favorably enhances the synthesis of the myofibrillar proteins involved in muscle contraction. Although some of the advantages gradually disappear when you stop working

> People who maintain a regular exercise routine have maximum bone density and strength.

out, the exercised bones are wider even several decades after the practice. This suggests that starting exercise from an early age can lead to greater and stronger bone life. Exercise has a positive impact on bones, and this may help increase osteocalcin levels, which is a proven and commonly used biochemical marker of bone formation. Regular exercising has been considered as a low-cost and safe non-pharmacological treatment for the preservation of musculoskeletal health.

Nevertheless, the effects of exercise on bones have so far been significantly lower in elderly people. The lack of significant changes in bone quality due to exercise in older people may be due to the fact that the body cannot exert as much force as we get older, or that bones are less resilient to the forces we generate. Throughout daily movements and exercise, forces acting on our bones have a great impact on the size, shape and strength of our bones. Lack of physical activity or a sedentary lifestyle can make the bones weaker and more likely to break, but staying physically active and doing activities such as running, soccer or playing tennis can help strengthen bones.

Exercise and muscles

Depending on the nature of the physical activity, exercise requires a sequence of prolonged muscle contractions, either long or short. Effects of exercise on muscles can be

What Happens to your Body when you Start Exercising Regularly?

considered short-term or immediate, both during and shortly after exercise, as well as long-term or lasting effects. When we exercise, the brain sends a message to the muscle fibres through the nerves. The fibres respond through contraction, which generates motion.

Exercises that require constant movement, such as rowing, walking or swimming, result in muscle fibres being rhythmically tightened and released. This cycle not only helps improve the movement of the body, but also promotes a *milking* action that helps move blood through the veins and back into the heart.

As iron-rich myoglobin fibres increase during aerobic exercise, it allows more oxygen to enter and be processed within the muscles. A larger number of capillaries[6], combined with an enhanced flow of blood to the muscles, improve muscle function and help strengthen muscles. So not only can your well-trained muscles retain more glycogen, but also burn fat more specifically for energy, maintaining glycogen stores.

Weight training is significantly important to improve your muscle mass, as you have possibly heard many times from your gym-goer friend. When a person continually challenges the muscles through exercise (mostly higher levels

---

[6]. Capillaries are tiny blood vessels connecting arteries to veins. These blood vessels carry oxygen and nutrients to individual cells throughout the body.

of resistance training or weight training) the size of muscles increases and becomes more defined or toned. This process is known as muscle hypertrophy. Strength training promotes muscle hypertrophy and helps increase muscle mass and often this is a long-term consequence of maintaining a regular fitness regime. Hypertrophy of the muscle occurs when muscle fibres are weakened or injured. The body replaces the weakened fibres by fusing them, which increases muscle mass and strengthens them. Several hormones, including testosterone and insulin, also play a major role in muscle repair and development.

When you follow a routine for your strength training, it is equally important to include a rest day in your schedule. In fact, rest days work as catalysts to your strength training. How, you may ask. When you train your muscles, you allow them to repair from the exertions caused by training. Muscle soreness which is a result of exertions due to high intensity training is a common occurrence among people who train regularly. Rest days help heal the soreness by repairing tissues, building and adapting skeletal muscles, and restoring fuel reserves in the body. Imagine when you have an injury in your hand and try to do regular activities with it. Unless you let it heal and get back to its normal condition, you will not be

> Your well-trained muscles burn fat more specifically for energy.

able to use it to its optimum potential. It could even worsen the condition. Hence, insufficient rest may slow down your gain and increase your risk of getting injured.

Experts recommend not carrying out weight training for two consecutive days on the same muscle group. When I mean resting for muscle growth, I would also like you to focus on maintaining a good night's sleep and a healthy diet. *It is imperative to get enough sleep and follow a balanced diet to improve muscle protein synthesis, muscle growth and promote muscle recovery.*

TAKEAWAYS

- The more mitochondria our cells have, the more strengthened the cells become and help improve overall health. Even minimal physical activities help expand the mitochondria in our cells rapidly. So, get started!
- Daily physical activity helps minimize the risk of neurodegenerative disorders and creates neuroprotective effects in our brain by protecting the fittest mitochondria.
- A moderate yet consistent exercise routine increases the volume of the hippocampus (the brain region responsible for memory) by 2% and reverses the deterioration associated with age by one to two years.
- High intensity interval training enhances protein synthesis in the muscles, which staves off the age-related internal deterioration.
- Strength training is the most effective way to increase muscle mass and improve overall body structure.

6
Motivation is Overrated in Fitness: Environment Matters More

> *You are the average of the five people you spend the most time with.*
>
> – Jim Rohn

The foot-ninja

Sweat drenched t-shirt, bottle full of electrolytes, a racing pulse, and sweet soreness in the legs. Not the regular list of things you would look forward to on a pleasant Saturday morning, right? Neither was it for Ranjith Krishan aka RK. But that was before he joined the running club.

A successful accountant, RK had focused on his career and family all his life, never giving much thought to exercise or fitness. As he scaled the corporate ladder, this negligence began to show, and he was soon tipping the scales at 110 kilos. He had begun to worry about his weight and had intermittently attempted morning walks and gym memberships to get it under control. However, he was unable to dedicate the requisite time for it.

In time, he accepted a position at ABC Corp, never imagining the momentous change awaiting him. He got acquainted with his co-workers, including Shyam, who was (and continues to be) a keen marathon runner. As they got talking, RK found that Shyam had already participated in two marathons that year and was preparing for yet another one. As the days passed, Shyam's running featured in a number of their casual conversations.

One day, RK asked Shyam how he found the time and enthusiasm to run so regularly. He also confessed that he had been trying to get into the habit of exercising but had not had any success so far. Shyam revealed that he was not alone in this. He had a group of runners who he ran regularly with, who were more like his friends now. He invited RK to come along for a couple of runs. RK took him up on the offer and tagged along with Shyam the next weekend.

RK had imagined a handful of people running around a park but was surprised to find that the group consisted of over twenty people from different walks of life and different age groups. They invited him to their WhatsApp group, where they communicated often about the runs, progress and achievements of the members. He found that they ran at least thrice a week and coaxed and goaded each other to be regular. Very soon, RK found himself looking forward to the runs. Initially, the company of interesting people and the camaraderie kept him going, but as the weeks passed, he began to enjoy the run. As he continued, he began to notice the physical and mental changes his effort in running had brought – the increased stamina, the weight loss and the improved focus in his day-to-day life. He started liking the new change in his lifestyle and slowly, running became a habit with him.

The things he had never imagined enjoying, became the things he looked forward to, even on a weekday! As RK said about his running habit:

"I don't think of skipping my run – whether it's for forty minutes or fifteen minutes, I run anyway.
I don't even have to think about choosing whether to run or not anymore.
No resistance.
No self-forcing.
No teeth-grinding. It's natural and a part of my daily life."

Fitness Habits

RK's story is an inspirational one. If you are committed to practice, it gets easier with time. And to make your workout a daily practice, the importance of social environment cannot be ignored. People change their behaviour to meet the demands of a particular social environment. We match up to the behaviour of the groups we mingle with, we tend to replicate the behaviour or actions that match our own interests and opinions, as did RK.

Humans are social beings and hence, our decisions are made based on our social interactions, personal relationships and physical environments, all influenced by the environment we are surrounded with. The truth is, if we are isolated, we very rarely make choices.

The social influence, which we call the environment, comes from the social groups we hang out with, people we follow on social media, family and coworkers, to name a few. External environmental cues can influence us in remarkable ways. Every day, we encounter social influence in its many forms. And nowadays, perceptions, communication, and behaviour affected by society are increasingly driven by technology. There are many explanations for why the environment broadly affects our thoughts and behaviour. One explanation for this is that we always want to fit in with friends

> When you start enjoying your workout, you won't have to force yourself to do it.

Motivation is Overrated in Fitness: Environment Matters More

and colleagues and prefer to be loved and respected by other members of that group. Often, for habits like fitness, social groups play an important role in driving our behaviour. We humans preserve a deep inclination towards rising to the key behaviour of the group we belong to. We develop habits to keep up with societal changes, we adjust our attitudes and behaviour to match the accepted norms of the groups we have close connections with, we love to be a part of the group we look up to, we love to raise our societal bars.

If we pull the examples from real-life situations together, it becomes easily understandable. Football team supporters willingly wear their team shirts to feel a part of the community. Friends wear identical clothes to feel a sense of belonging to the same group and ensure that they share common ideas. A student may change his or her behaviour in class to suit that of other students or watch a particular TV show because classmates at college talk about it.

As Jonah Berger said in his book *Invisible Influence: The Hidden Forces that Shape Behaviour,* "Our likes and dislikes are often driven in subtle and surprising ways by people around us." If a lot of students pick up some items at lunch, that might make you more likely to pick up similar items. When a bunch of your friends play a particular mobile game, it sounds cool, and to be a part of the same group, you want to join in too.

The magnetic pull of social environment

Environment is the catalyst that helps us make the routines consistent and rewards achievable. Numerous psychological studies on human behaviour have shown that we imitate most of the behaviour from the people we mingle with or follow the most. This also leads to the conclusion that when you surround yourself with people who follow a certain behavioural or habitual pattern, you tend to adopt similar behaviour or habits to feel accepted in the group, which eventually encourages you to replicate similar habitual patterns.

Environment is something that shapes our behaviour and helps us build better habits in the long run. Though the effect of the environment may affect us in so many other ways as well, we will talk about how the environment is a crucial factor in shaping our behaviour in a good way. The truth is that whether picking up a good habit or getting rid of a bad one, the importance of our environment can never be ignored. Along with shaping our behaviour, our environment also moulds our emotions, belief system, attitude, our inspiration and the standards and expectations we set for ourselves. Learning is always more interesting when we have a community to learn with. Just like in any classroom setting, having a support group in our close setup has an extremely powerful impact when they share similar goals and vibes.

Motivation is Overrated in Fitness: Environment Matters More

Our environment is like a magnet; it attracts our conscience and leads us to do things as people around us do.

Judgments and decisions are not always ideal. Rather, they are focused on the psychological concepts of how people interpret knowledge and process it. In 1958, Harvard psychologist Herbert Kelman proposed the social influence theory,[7] where he mentioned that human beings are influenced by the behaviour of a group because it is intrinsically rewarding. We adopt the induced behaviour of the group since it matches our value system and becomes a part of our own belief system. This also means that the changes in the adopted behaviour are permanent. Another research carried out by Cialdini and his colleagues suggests that humans are profoundly driven to establish and maintain meaningful social relationships with others as we tend to change our opinions and behaviours in order to follow social norms, even if the majority decision is against our personal preference.

We, as social creatures, are always on the lookout for behaviours, actions or attitudes that we can adopt to enhance our image. We usually use people to guide us and we use the influencers as a signal of information. It is our natural

> Learning is always more interesting when we have a community to learn with.

---

7. Kelman's social influence theory: https://scholar.harvard.edu/files/hckelman/files/Compliance_identification_and_internalization.pdf

Fitness Habits

tendency to mimic the people we like and the ones who we are surrounded with. We have evolved by imitating others and subconsciously capturing the thoughts of each other by the mirror neuron[8].

Since the time we were born, we practice mimicking either our parents or closest family members. Without it, there is no emotional bonding. When we grew up, we realized the importance to be a part of a group and how important it is to be accepted by others. It creates a sense of satisfaction to know that the people who we are surrounded with have made similar decisions or choices as it validates our own choices and establishes our recognition as a part of the group.

We mostly imitate the habits of people from three major groups that we associate ourselves with:

1. Family
2. Friends or people we like
3. The praised or the role models

We are likely to reflect the behaviours or habits of these three types of people in our life and each group has a major influence in shaping our habits. Fitness habits, in particular.

---

8. Mirror neurons are a type of brain cells that respond equally when we perform an action and when we witness someone else perform the same action.

Motivation is Overrated in Fitness: Environment Matters More

1. The family

The family is the most influencing factor for us. It forms an environment in which we evolve, shape our personality, acquire values, and develop attitudes and opinions on various subjects, including fitness. Habits like fitness are strongly influenced by the members of our family.

Numerous studies have shown the role of family in shaping our healthy habits like healthy and unhealthy eating, physical activity, smoking, alcohol consumption and insufficient sleep. The influence of our family can be so intense that even though we are not consciously trying, we may pick up on the behaviour of our family members. We are more likely to eat more veggies if we are habituated to eating veggies since childhood; we are more likely to do better at sports if one of our parents or family members are closely associated with any kind of sports. If your wife or husband is a fitness freak, you tend to follow some kind of fitness activity and eat healthy, even if you have never been a fitness follower before.

2. Friends and people we like

One of the reasons why we want to be friends with people we like is that the more we like them and approve of them, the more likely we are to maintain strong relationships with

> Habits like fitness are strongly influenced by the members of our family.

Fitness Habits

them. It creates significant improvements that help us grow and compete. We mimic the behaviours of people we like because we admire them and prefer to inculcate their habits, sometimes unconsciously. This is true – we draw a part of our sense of identity and self-esteem from our friends and the groups we mingle with.

Typically, being with people we like and people we consider as friends leads to positive feelings because we eventually view them as a part of our community. As a result, we also see ourselves in a positive light when there is a resemblance of habit traits. When we are with our group of friends or with our favorite bunch of people, we level up to match the performance of the group. Psychologists call this *social facilitation*. Closest friends or groups can help us do things that we might not do otherwise. So, how can we set our environment to encourage ourselves to be fitter and make healthy choices just by placing our near and dear ones in and around us?

Sometimes others seem to be motivating, whereas in the same situation, if we are placed alone, we might lack the motivation and act differently. The wisdom of crowds, of course, is often a much-celebrated phenomenon. It is unlikely to find someone who is not influenced by anyone in his whole life. For example, merely working out with friends makes us work out as regularly and put in the reps, even when it gets harder, or running with our friend makes us run faster.

Motivation is Overrated in Fitness: Environment Matters More

We like being connected to others who are similar to us in some way. What is interesting is that others often influence us before we realize that we are being influenced by them. People we like lead us to work harder and do better, but at the same time, it instigates us to outperform them and be better than them. While we like to adopt the behaviours of others, habits like fitness can be an interesting example to show how we try to perform similar to the person we are mimicking or how, sometimes, we wish to surpass them.

When we work out with our friends, we want to match our pace with them because we do not want to look inferior. As a general rule, having someone else to compare ourselves with matters a lot, and this, as a matter of fact, makes it easier to develop habits like fitness. We want to match pace and never want to fall back.

3. The praised or the role models
We prefer to obtain social acceptance to create rewarding relationships with others and to boost our self-esteem in the process. Mimicking the most-liked personalities offers us an opportunity to earn more respect, admiration and status by scaling up our habits to their levels. We try to copy the habits of people we praise or look up to, because we like to see

> When we work out with our friends, we want to match up or do better.

Fitness Habits

ourselves in their position. We like to be included in the elite group.

Seeing your favorite person climb the ladder of success makes you follow their steps; you replicate the eating habits of people who are considered as nutrition experts or knowledgeable in the nutrition field; you love to cook the way your favorite chef or baker cooks; you even like to copy the writing style of your favorite authors. We like to attain the skills and expertise of people we admire. Our desire to obtain the social approval of others, a desire to make a correct choice, and a desire to keep a positive self-concept leads us to copy the people we consider as successful. Hence, mimicking them serves as a type of intrinsic motivation to follow their path.

We also love to identify with someone who seems to lead a perfect life. Consciously, we want to become great and follow the same habits that make the great ones great. We all have our favorites on social media and in our personal lives; these are the people we idolize for different reasons. Seeing your idol sweating out in the gym may make you choose fitness. When you see your favorite fashion icon choosing particular brands for clothes, skincare or shoes, you tend to eye those brands. Watching the videos of fitness idols on social media influence us to follow those particular workouts, techniques, or even buy the same fitness gears and outfits too.

In order to earn the same prestige as our most-liked people, we tend to fabricate our habits in accordance to the people, who are popular. We want to look popular, act like popular people, and speak like them. The thing is, it is more likely to gain trust and respect if it is associated with somebody well-known, popular or successful. We like to get approval from others when we engage in behaviours of which others approve. As a result, to build, maintain and evaluate the quality of our relationships with others, we use approval and liking cues.

Group workout – where *reward* meets fun

A qualitative, purposeful sampling study was conducted to explore the experiences of adults who participated in regular group exercises. A Nielsen's study of more than 3,000 participants from group fitness classes around the world has revealed that more than 85% of their overall members attend group classes twice a week. Among them, 43% of the members attended group classes four times a week. According to the study, group fitness classes motivate people to keep going back to the workout classes and enjoy the healthy push that the members derive from the group of people who have similar goals.

> Working out in a group can help you change a fitness routine into a fitness habit.

Fitness Habits

Another research was conducted by Dr Jinger Gottschall of Penn State University among a group of 25 sedentary men and women between the age group of 25-40 years to understand the impact of group fitness. During the 30 weeks of the fitness program, the participants were gradually introduced to different forms of exercise and time spent on each form of exercise was increased step by step in order to reduce fatigue and improve commitment to the curriculum. The assessment after the end of the program was a surprising revelation. The body fat percentage and cholesterol level reduced significantly, and this led them to stick to their fitness program almost at the rate of 99%.

There are a number of researches that testify to the importance of a group indulgence in helping change a routine to a habit. When you take a step towards making fitness a lifestyle choice, the environment you choose to belong to plays a crucial role in sticking to the routine, which in turn, becomes a motivational factor to form a fitness habit.

In 2017, Gympik conducted a behavioural study among the general masses to understand the impact of group exercising. The study was conducted among male and female subjects, aging between 20-40 years who were in the beginner to intermediate stages of fitness. The findings were quite insightful and can provide a valuable framework for understanding the consequences of exercising with a group. Additionally, the positive behavioural signs among the participants can also be used to promote fitness and encourage more people to make fitness a part of their lifestyle. This study revealed that nearly 56% of the participants found the group classes more sustainable because being a part of a bigger community makes the workout look easier and more doable.

Moreover, a group of people enhances the feeling of togetherness, and doing something ambitious while supporting each other is a bonus that keeps them coming back to exercising. Among the younger group of people, around 48% stated that the most compelling reason to go back to group classes is the energy sync. The energy and positivity that come together in a group class is addictive and people who mostly attend the group classes said that mingling and working out with people of different fitness levels made them feel accepted without being judged.

The general finding among the participants who were consistent with group classes, which was nearly 62% of the participants, expressed that staying connected with people and interacting with them enhanced a sense of social and moral bonding. Hence, according to the study, the social factor of group exercise can be considered as one of the most compelling and therapeutic points that works as a motivator.

Fitness Habits

Apart from these, there are a few important yet powerful factors that convince beginners or weight watchers to choose group classes. Adira Shah, a 32-year-old HR professional said, "Group exercise builds a healthy peer pressure. Seeing other people do the same workout as you, even when it is tough, makes you surpass your level and do the best you can. It gives you a different kind of motivation and improves your performance when you think, 'if they can do it, I can do that too'. Although there is a competitive atmosphere around, it feels supportive."

Another perception that adds value to group workout classes is that each class is structured by a certified trainer. While trainers guide members with each set of exercises, certain trainers exude contagious motivational behaviour that encourages people to take their workout up a notch. The VP of a reputed MNC, Nikhil Bhardwaj, emphasized, "I like group classes over one-to-one personal training programs – be it yoga or HIIT or TRX. I like to sweat out with a group of people who have become friends now. We sweat together, struggle together but do it anyway, even when it gets tough. The trainers guide each member pretty well. Also, a structured class with exercises of different intensity is the best."

> Group exercise can be considered as one of the most compelling and therapeutic points that works as a motivator.

Motivation is Overrated in Fitness: Environment Matters More

Nearly 62% of the beginners prefer to go to group classes as they do not need to stick to boring cardio like walking on a treadmill or running or structure their workout from sources such as YouTube or social media without knowing what fits their routine.

Additionally, almost 48% of the participants felt that the feel-good communication and societal bond they created after talking to people before and after the workout was beneficial for their mental health as it improved their confidence and cognitive function when they mingled with people from different walks of life and shared a connection beyond their regular life.

Moreover, workouts with a group improve the level of consistency as they involve a certain level of commitment. "If you happen to miss a workout or stay inconsistent, you are sure to be noticed by your workout buddies, including the instructor. This gives you a feeling of missing out on the classes when others went a step ahead. This kind of positive peer pressure can help stave off the urges to skip a workout," says 20-year-old BCA student, Namrata.

How to design a favorable environment

Human behaviour is shaped by the invisible hand of nature, that is, our environment. There is a general human tendency to believe that our habits are the by-product of our motivational

Fitness Habits

talent and efforts. Such attributes certainly are significant in a human being. But the surprising truth is, in the long run, our personal features appear to become overshadowed by the environment we are surrounded with. We tend to blame the lack of motivation and determination in our lives to a lack of progress. Whether you are a beginner or at an intermediate stage in fitness, there will be days when you will not feel like showing up and cannot bring yourself to do anything besides lying on the couch and relaxing. No matter what stage you are in, monotony will creep in, your energy level will be the lowest of low and the challenges will overshadow your motivation.

Whether we realize it or not, our environment is constantly influencing us to do what we do or do not do. Our environment delivers the cues which trigger certain behaviours. When you respond to the cue that leads to a similar routine over a period of time, you create a habit. Psychology says, as humans, we often choose the path of least resistance, as it saves energy and willpower. And to make this process work, we constantly look out to design an environment that makes our routine easy to follow and effectively help in forming a habit.

The behaviours that help you form your habits determine the simplest choices or rather the decisions you make every day in your life. Imagine if you were asked to travel ten kilometres to reach your gym after work, where you do not

Motivation is Overrated in Fitness: Environment Matters More

have any company, and after an hour of workout you have to travel back home, crossing the same distance. It is obvious that you will not feel excited about your workout and miss a few days in a week for some or the other reason. The reasons may range from extended work hours for important deliverables to reaching home early to attend a party, or very simply – you feel lazy to travel that far and work out in such a far-flung and monotonous vicinity.

The struggle is real, no doubt!

Now imagine that you join a gym that is closer to your workplace as well as your house. You have a couple of colleagues who go to the same gym and you have a group of workout buddies who come to the gym at the same time as you do.

The same person doing similar physical exertion at two different places with two different environment set-ups. Often, our decisions that require the fuel of constant motivation and willpower are bound to fail as we run out of these quite easily. When we feel that our daily 'to do' list requires a humongous effort and truckloads of motivation to accomplish, we tend to procrastinate it often. Because motivation and willpower are only a short-term strategy to make things work. They disappear the moment challenges arrive.

If you are a writer, you cannot write only when you feel motivated. A student cannot study only when he is motivated. An entrepreneur cannot put efforts into his business only

Fitness Habits

when he is motivated. Hence, something concrete is required to solve this behavioural alteration, i.e. habit. Your habits run you on an autopilot mode and make it easier for you to stick to the goals you have set for yourself, without waiting for motivation to fuel them.

Even though you set out to stick to your fitness habit with the best of intentions, if your environment decides differently, you fail to stick to it. The way our environment is set up determines how we act in different situations. While we cannot alter the situations we are in, creating a conducive environment makes it easier to find the cue and follow the routine without even having to think about staying motivated. I call it *'designing a favourable environment'* – it can help you build better habits and stick to them even when you are low on motivation and willpower.

Designing your environment works as an amazing tool to develop your fitness habit. Linking your cues with your environment makes your fitness habit the default choice. If your environment has cues that prompt you to make healthier choices, you do not have to draw motivation to perform the task. When the cues for your fitness habit are right in front of you, making the decision becomes easier. For example, if you want to go to work out every day

> Designing your environment works as an amazing tool to develop your fitness habit.

Motivation is Overrated in Fitness: Environment Matters More

after office, carrying your workout clothes and pre-workout snacks to work make it easier for you to go for a workout. Associating your workout clothes and pre-workout snacks with your workout serve as powerful cues to follow your workout routine.

In the previous chapters, I have discussed how habits work and how, when you are in sync with your habits, you do what your habits make you do – you become the compilation of the habits that you have practiced over a period of time. If you want to improve your chances of being fitter, you need to create an environment that helps you do more of it. The fundamental objective is to establish a potent environment in which your fitness choice occurs effortlessly.

Now the question is – how to design your environment so that it supports your intended actions and behaviour to help form your fitness habit? Perhaps, adapting to the current environment is not always enough to develop your fitness habits. In that case, you must design a completely new environment. Most of the time, forming a new habit requires designing your environment in a way that makes your habit easier to follow. This is where environmental design comes into play. When you design your environment, you choose to do a set of activities in a particular way

> To make your fitness habit work, you need to redesign your environment.

Fitness Habits

till they fall into the default state and run on automation. For that, we need little environmental reminders to make our cues inevitable.

We are constantly choosing our habits, from good to bad, that lead to our successes or failures. If we give in to the environment we presently are in, we might not always succeed in fitting our fitness habit in our day-to-day life. And there comes the struggle. Simply put, the environment in which you live dictates more than you might wish. To battle the constant struggle to fit into the existing environment might not always work when your fitness habit is in the inception stage.

Meanwhile, to make your fitness habit work, you need a redesigning of your environment. If you want to become healthier, more consistent with your fitness routine and upgrade your fitness habit, start by building an environment that prepares the ground for you, one that ensures consistency and makes better results over a long duration easier.

But the question is – How can you design your environment so that your fitness habit becomes easier to develop and maintain? I have listed seven ways to make your fitness habit easy to form and difficult to resist in the next few pages. I have followed the same, and I would like you to follow these rules to make your fitness habit seem wonderful and something that you look forward to every day.

1. Start hanging out with fitness enthusiasts

If you want to write better, you hang out with people who are experts in the field and discuss how to improve your writing skills. If you want to invest in your startup, you mingle with people who have already done that in the past or who have better business skills than you. When you want to develop a fitness habit, choose to hang out with people who have been working out for a while. Not only will you have company to discuss the difficult parts of your fitness journey, you will end up getting the right solutions to overcome them as well.

Moreover, people who have mastered the art of fitness can be an immense source of motivation when you are in dire need of it. Revving up your fitness journey can be frustrating at times. We lose hope, we get stuck, we give up sometimes, but having a buddy who you can share your thoughts about your fitness goals with makes you responsible to follow your routine and helps you stay accountable to your fitness progress. After all, it sucks to look weaker in front of others, and if you have a fitness enthusiast buddy, you will rather avoid being someone who is weak.

2. Design your workout flow

Determine which physical activity you wish to continue doing over a period of time. Beginners can start from the most basic exercises like running or jogging or even walking, just to start

Fitness Habits

off. This can help you continue with your fitness habit and eventually set up a healthy relationship with fitness. Figure out when you can fit that activity in your day – early in the morning, in the afternoon or in the evening.

Once you are done with choosing your move, prioritize your schedule and look for the cues that can drive you to continue with the routine. For example, if you are planning to go for a jog early in the morning, go to bed early so that you do not have to hit the snooze button repeatedly when the alarm rings. If the morning coffee gives you a kick to start your day, have that and go ahead with your jogging. For some people, morning rituals like having a glass of warm water and doing a few stretches are the cues that drive them to follow the routine of a morning walk. Design your fitness habit in a way that it fits into the flow of the regular patterns of your day and eventually becomes a part of your daily rituals.

3. Make your cues visible
The changes you want to create in your routine should stick to your mind day in and day out. Stick a calendar somewhere visible and start ticking off the days you go for a workout or morning jog, keep your workout gear close to you and within your reach so that when you wake up, you get to notice them. These serve as visible cues and stand as reminders for your

workout session. It bothers us to ignore the visible cues and makes it difficult to miss the routine. This works as a simple strategy that encourages progress and is a fast way to adapt to the environment to support your objectives. Keep your focus on creating obvious cues throughout the day that lead to fueling your fitness habit.

4. *Choose the people you want to work out with or love to mingle with*

As discussed earlier in the chapter about the motivational effects of a group, humans are social animals and they love to spend time with people who share similar bonds, interests and goals. Going for a jog alone might need constant motivation, but when you have a couple of friends accompanying you, it feels easily doable and the temporary lethargy to dismiss a day's workout becomes much easier to handle. Research says that if you are trying to grow into the person you want to be, it is important to surround yourself with people who share the values you strive to achieve.

Being in fitness for more than a decade, I have seen people moving to gyms where their old friends from previous gyms, colleagues or other acquaintances work out. People prefer to have a convenient environment and

> Keep your focus on creating obvious cues that lead to fuelling your fitness habit.

familiar faces when they work out. It provides active social time and builds in accountability. You need this support when you are trying to develop your fitness habit, the best approach is to choose an environment that works in your favour and going to the same gym your friends or your colleagues go to. This makes it easier to drive your fitness routine.

5. Seek help

Whenever we try to change our usual routine, it affects the people around us in some or the other way. You will find a few who are excited about your choice in making fitness a habit, but there will be a few who will raise an eyebrow, questioning the need for change in your lifestyle. In the case of fitness, when deriving sheer motivation is in itself a big task, tackling the pushbacks are even harder when you least expect them. It is crucial for you to make your priorities clear to the people who are important to you and get their support when you need it while fitting into a new routine such as fitness.

Let's assume you are the one who usually sits with your kid, helping him with his homework every evening. But now that you plan to go for a jog after work, would your husband/wife/partner take your place in helping your kid with his homework? At work, you may be the one who gives extra hours to finish a project on time, but if you need to leave half an hour early to join your fitness training, will your colleagues extend a helping hand? Seek help from people who support your choice, at home or at work. This can be done when you are starting to incorporate a fitness routine in your daily life. Seeking help at the right time not only helps you become more productive of the time you are spending on a particular task, whether it's at home or at work, but also makes you responsible for maintaining a serious approach to your fitness routine.

6. Link your workout with indirect rewards

According to researchers, identifying an intrinsic reward helps make a fitness habit easier to develop. For example, extending your social network and getting to know more people may be indirectly rewarding. Who does not like to be a part of a group that motivates them to be a better and healthier person!

There are days when I miss my workouts unintentionally due to some meetings at work or other engagements. At the end of the day, I receive at least ten messages from my fellow gym goers asking me the reason for not going to the gym. I like the fact that the people I work out with check on me and I feel connected with them. I feel guilty for missing my workout when I see that other people are continuing with theirs. It is our natural tendency to hate lagging behind.

When you feel you are missing out, it naturally urges you to get back on the wagon.

If you have a bunch of gym partners who encourage you not to skip your workout, challenge you when you want to give up, push you to make healthier lifestyle choices when you plan otherwise, make you stay updated with the latest fitness gadgets, gear, and workout wear to ramp up your fitness couture, you are more likely to stay motivated about your fitness routine. Connect your fitness with such indirect rewards and you are more likely to stick to your fitness habit.

7. Make fitness easy to access

Wanting something done is not enough. If you want to make progress in fitness, form a fitness habit. And to form your fitness habit, you need an environment that gets you closer to it. Choosing a gym that is close by or creating a circle where your fitness habit is considered as normal behaviour, make it easier to follow and stick to.

While giving up is the easier option to choose, we always tend not to. And if not giving up becomes easier to pursue, it becomes irresistible. Your habits change depending on how easily accessible they are to you. It is difficult to give a miss to the chocolate bar resting in the front

> Working out with others can be a positive motivation for working out.

cabinet of the refrigerator for an apple that is lying somewhere in the vegetable drawer, draped in a brown paper bag. If you want to include fruits in your diet, keep them in a place where they are always visible to you and stand as a prominent cue to pick them up. If you want to make healthier food choices, stop buying foods that are unhealthy, high-caloric or packaged. Fill your refrigerator and kitchen cupboards with healthy alternatives so that unhealthy foods are out of your reach and you are surrounded with only healthier options. Similarly, when your workout place is closer to your office or home, you are more likely to show up than give it a miss. We like to continue anything that is easily accessible and causes less friction in our day-to-day life. Therefore, easy accessibility helps make habit-forming so much simpler.

TAKEAWAYS

- Hang out with people who make your fitness habit seem like a normal lifestyle choice. We try to match our pace with fitness-minded people because we do not want to look inferior.
- Motivation and willpower are not consistent and reliable sources to fuel the fitness habit. Design a favourable environment that makes the cue prominent and helps you follow the routine without constantly looking for motivation.
- Group fitness classes help improve consistency. Socializing is one of the most compelling and therapeutic factors that works as a motivator to maintain a commitment to fitness.
- Establish your environment in a way that your fitness routine falls effortlessly into the flow of your daily routines. This helps in shaping your fitness habits.
- Choosing a gym that is easily accessible or having fitness enthusiast friends help make your fitness habit easier to follow and stick to.

7
The Personal Trainer – An Anchor for your Fitness

> *When performance is measured, performance improves. When performance is measured and reported, the rate of improvement accelerates.*
> – Thomas S. Monson

A colleague of mine, Shree, is an absolute charmer and an amazing team player. She always has a smile on her face and is a happy-go-lucky girl who is full of confidence. A marathoner, a trekker, and a writer, this 28-year-old marketing professional has redefined courage and dedication and proved that perseverance is not for the faint-hearted. Looking at her present demeanour, it is difficult to fathom the girl she used to be.

It was in the year 2016 that she was at her wit's end, struggling to manage the life of a normal human being.

That was when she was diagnosed with hypothyroidism and hormonal complications. She hit rock bottom as she realized that all her health complications were fuelling her mental trauma. She was stuck in the never-ending, vicious cycle of making poor lifestyle choices. She felt that she was merely surviving and not living her life to the fullest.

Running from pillar to post, consulting health specialists with lists of prescriptions, medicines and no sustainable results had left her exhausted and exasperated. It was a regular day in mid-April 2016 when she fell sick at work. She was gasping for breath and in the next moment, she remembered that her colleagues had gathered around and rushed her to the hospital. She fainted and her blood pressure was insanely high.

She stood perplexed when the doctor handed her the prescription and added a few more medicines to her already extensive list of medicines. She was prescribed to follow a healthy lifestyle, better food habits and some sort of fitness activity to keep her weight in check. She had her back to the wall, as her frustration started piling up with each passing minute. Her fear of getting stuck with a poor health condition started clouding her mind.

> The fear of losing everything often piles up in our mind when we face health challenges.

What happened that day was not merely an accident; it was a critical juncture that led her to rummage through the montage of thoughts about where her life was heading. The fear of losing everything was piling up in her mind. She could either turn, muster up her courage to make changes and live a healthier life, or live the life she abhorred. She could either win it over or live the rest of her life as a victim of poor health conditions. It was the moment when she felt – *not here again*! In her words, "That was the moment I realized what misery could feel like. It came through like a hard punch in the gullet. It rocked my world, and I could feel something boiling in my body."

When she spoke to me about her health issues, she was in a quandary about how to start a fitness routine and position it in her all-sloppy lifestyle. Being from a conservative family in Rajasthan, fitness was the last option in her life. She was uncertain about what she could do to start a fitness routine that would help her, what kind of workouts to choose from the vast array of options, who to reach out to for help, and so on and so forth. The only fitness options she could think of were either running or walking. Not sure about what would suit her, she joined a gym. But for her, that proved to be a disappointing experience. The drills at the gym left her heart trembling with a strange anxiety coupled with boredom, uncertainty and an undetermined path that was defined only by knowledge that she had compiled from the internet. It was during those days when she was struggling to find a way to at least try to make some changes in her lifestyle that she spoke to me.

She said, "I have tried walking and jogging. I could barely make it a priority due to other engagements in life."

"I feel the need of the hour is your health, and it's probably the only choice you are left with," I said.

"I have recently started walking, but I am still not able to make it a daily routine. I also know that just walking is not the solution to my problem. I need to do something more to stabilize my weight. I need a push, and honestly, I have no clue how to get help," she said hesitantly.

"It's normal for a beginner to feel that way. What I feel is you should consider taking personal training, either at home or at a gym," I said, hoping she would find a better solution.

"I don't think I can cope with the thought of gym and personal training. It's a matter of a lot of money too," said Shree.

"Well, there are two concerns at the same time – your health and money. You have to choose to prioritize," I said.

"Even if I hire a personal trainer, I don't know whether I will be able to commit to that for long. It'll be the same story once I stop taking personal training."

"Look, there's a reason why you need a personal trainer now. You need someone to teach you the type of exercises that are right for you. And most importantly, you need an expert to guide you in the right direction and set realistic milestones for you. Someone who tracks your progress, encourages you to follow your workout routine every day, someone who not only helps you prioritize your workout but also keeps you motivated for the rewards you are looking for. And that's the job of a personal trainer."

I continued, "Let me ask you this – Do you look for a solution through an online video when you have an acute case of vertigo or hypertension? No, right? It's like going to the specialist when you have a certain health issue. It's wise to consult someone who knows about fitness more than you do, and a trainer is the one who fits the category. Do not second guess that."

"Sounds logical, I agree. Here I am, grasping at straws, and you are the only one to help me find a good personal trainer," she said.

And I did help her find a qualified personal trainer who knows his job and is known for being dedicated to his clients' progress. A few months later, with the help of the trainer, she could rescue herself from falling prey to the destiny of poor health. She was now a different Shree – someone who was facing her health challenges like a boss. There was a huge boost in her self-esteem. She has become more enthusiastic about her life, her workout and is positive beyond anything. Her weight loss has been an outward reflection of the

Fitness Habits

healthier state of her mind and all this happened because she chose to make fitness and health her priority, chose to stay accountable for her progress by hiring a personal trainer.

Fitness for a beginner may seem overwhelming, no doubt. It can be challenging and confusing at the same time. It is a journey from dragging yourself to work out to enjoying every drop of sweat dripping off your body. Depending on the complexity of the task, our mind categorizes it as difficult or easy.

Let's admit that when we think about fitness, most of us are uncertain about what it means to us. The society we live in, our past experiences with fitness, and our knowledge about it have a direct influence on how we perceive fitness. And most of the time, it feels like a gruelling ordeal to push through these ingrained beliefs, especially the ones that are associated with fear of failure.

But the truth is, when you have a specified intention in mind and a guide, you are able to live and work intentionally towards achieving it. When people want to take up fitness, they want to work out to be healthier, manage their stress, lose weight and, most importantly, they want to feel excited about their fitness training.

> Fitness for a beginner may seem overwhelming in the beginning.

Our society has everything idealized for us – from the right body shape to the right complexion to the right career choices. The fitness choices too are not spared. My earliest memories of fitness are those from Ara, Bihar. The go-to options for fitness, as I have always observed, have been either morning walks or jogging or any kind of sport. Moreover, jogging or walking are recommended for those who are suffering from any kind of lifestyle-related diseases such as diabetes, hypertension, heart-related issues and so on. Though walking is favoured to be a universal exercise choice for most because it is the easiest form of fitness, it is revered as the sovereign remedy for all health problems. As I have discussed in the previous chapters, we are more likely to follow any fitness choice that is easy to do and maintain. It is also relevant to say that we tend to avoid the fitness choices that require us to go out of our comfort zones.

There is very little possibility that one can go wrong with walking, but if the same person is asked to run or do home workouts, they might become sceptical and never do it. The threat of failing at sustaining a different kind of workout may lead them to avoid working out altogether. Choosing any fitness option that requires extra effort in learning on your own initiative makes fitness look like a huge commitment and, sometimes, punishment. In general, developing a fitness habit requires a clear vision. From a desire to live a healthy life to solving a medical problem, the purpose of forming a

Fitness Habits

fitness habit is linked to a deep desire or a problem that we want to get rid of. Most of the time, in the case of fitness, people lack clarity and are unsure about when and how to take action. Therefore, for people like Shree, fitness remains a domain that is out of their comfort zone.

Fitness is as much about following the right guidance as setting the right environment. Forming any good habit that you want to fit into your lifestyle not only requires your constant conscious effort, but also a step-by-step guide to follow through. This simply makes it easier to stick to a predetermined plan and requires no decision making when it is time to take action. This way, you stay motivated and excited to stick to the routine and crave for the reward. As psychologists say, humans are motivated about something which is challenging yet tolerable and we get motivated when we see frequent signals of progress. With fitness, we often bite off more than we can chew, and this stalls our progress. What I mean is, we do not set a realistic fitness goal or stick to a consistent plan; this is a common issue among beginners – to either do too less or go overboard with their workouts.

> Fitness is as much about following the right guidance as setting the right environment.

As it has been rightly said, to be better at anything is to get better every day. When you make progress, you want to keep going; but when you break progress, you want to stop. Too often, we let our impulses and expectations send us into such a state of frenzy that we want to solve our problems all at once, rather than taking the first step to make small changes. We expect too much in too little time and hence fail too early. On the flip side, you would love to follow an expert who can add value through knowledge, variety, motivation and, most importantly, accountability while guiding you through the process. One of the greatest challenges I have seen is maintaining awareness of what we are doing and why. This one fact is clear, that fitness improves everything, from bringing change in the way you look to adopting a healthy lifestyle. The quality of lifestyle is so integral to our happiness and better health that improving it even a little makes a remarkable difference in how much we can accomplish. This explains why making fitness a habit is never a waste of time and effort, but an immensely impactful way to improve the quality of life.

Here is the unfortunate reality – fitness, though has numerous benefits, is being ignored by many. Lifestyle-related diseases continue to rise around the world due to lack of any consistent fitness routine in our daily life. Fitness is a preventive medicine but without knowledgeable trainers, fitness is still out of reach for the masses. Whether you prefer to workout at home or at the gym, a personal trainer works as a catalyst to your fitness routine and makes your fitness journey a satisfying learning process. The strategy, of course, when you wish to scale up your fitness game, is to have a trainer or instructor who is qualified enough to walk you through the routine while showing you the way towards steady gains in fitness.

Every practice is a learning process

This is a common question among many – Why should I hire a personal trainer when I can search online and find thousands of videos for weight loss, weight gain, six-pack abs and whatnot? When people ask me this, my response is simple: Do you think you can learn engineering through online videos without knowing anything about the subject?

As a beginner in fitness, when you are in the early phases of your fitness journey, you may sometimes wonder whether you are sufficiently equipped for it. This is the phase where you need proper guidance, knowledge on the dos and don'ts of fitness, right postures, how different workouts impact your body type, etc. These cannot be learned from online videos. The internet today is filled with over-promising stories of quick fixes that, if not used with caution, may compromise your overall health. Unfortunately, we take our health for granted until something goes wrong. We try out different workouts without knowing the fundamentals, we start random diet plans, jump from one diet or workout routine to the other, too fast, until our body gives up. We get hurt, feel like a failure and blame it all on fitness. A personal trainer is a pillar to take you through your insecurities, struggles, your fitness goal, and help you nurture your motivation to achieve it.

Be it fitness, life, relationship or work, anything we try to master depends on knowing the fundamentals and practicing it consistently. It is simple and straightforward – *you get exactly what you put your efforts into*.

I love this quote by the American dancer, choreographer and author Twyla Tharp in her book, *The Creative Habit: Learn It and Use It for Life* – "Do them anyway – you can never spend enough time on the basics." It may sound ho-hum, but the truth in it is vast and to the point. Therefore, when you follow an inconsistent fitness routine or get swayed by fad diets, you only set yourself up for disappointment. Your personal trainer is the designated one who can help you learn the basics, design a fitness plan especially curated for you, and help you maintain a lifestyle that you can follow for the long haul.

> A personal trainer is a pillar to take you through your insecurities and struggles, to your fitness goal.

Forming your fitness habit requires starting from small changes every day, from preparing your mind to go for a workout, to get ready for another day. You need simple changes that fit into your lifestyle easily and rev up the speed when you are flexible enough with the current one. Slow and steady actions often take you a step closer to success because it keeps you motivated and reduces the fear of failure. If you are a beginner, it's the personal trainer who helps chalk out the plan and walks you through the path.

Hiring a personal trainer is bewildering. As I said earlier, everyone with a basic knowledge in fitness is a fitness trainer and nutrition expert these days. Plus, social media has ramified them based on the number of followers they have rather than their expertise. Though expending on a personal trainer can be the best possible investment you can think of to get better fitness results, most of us are leery about the results it may get us. Most of the time, it is about whether we will get the body we want within 'X' months, will we lose fat by this time, and so on.

You need to know that fitness isn't a magic pill. Just the way other thing need time to be learned and mastered, fitness isn't any different. A personal trainer can drive you towards what you want to achieve. If you are new to fitness, the right thing to do is to know how small you can start with and go ahead with making smaller improvements every day. From knowing the right workouts to implementing the right techniques, everything is just correctly measured according to your fitness level. The doubts you may have when you start your fitness journey can be addressed in the best possible way by someone who is an expert in the field.

You may be a beginner or a pro, but the importance of a personal trainer cannot be denied when you need to take your fitness to the next level. The first choice of anyone who has just started working out is, most of the time, workout videos they see online. While the workout videos are intended to be done without any help, knowing the basics is crucial to follow any workout. In fitness, if your form is not right while exercising, then you are at an increased risk of injury as well as failing to achieve your goals, since nothing destroys a dream like a ten-week long recommended bed rest because of injury. A personal trainer can fit into this situation and bridge the gap between you and your goal by teaching you the right exercises with the right postures that get you maximum benefits.

It would not be wrong to say that almost 80% of people who join a gym quit within two to three months because they don't know where to go further from where they started. A fitness trainer can not only help you with your workout step by step, an experienced trainer can also make a huge difference to your training program – from

> A personal trainer can take you through the fitness journey, step by step.

creating a personalized fitness plan to helping you learn the fundamentals of your workout routine.

The role of a good personal trainer in making your fitness journey a successful one is ample as he will be the one watching you closely while you perform every move and make sure that you do it right. There is nothing more important than following the right ways when you are a learner and to keep moving in the direction that helps you optimize your performance. Sometimes, it is the minor tweak or maybe the slightest technique, and I can tell you, it makes a huge difference in your performance when you follow through.

Each body is different, and when it comes to exercise, the abilities and requirements of everyone are different too. This could be anything from having an old injury requiring special exercises to curing any health issues that demand specific numbers on the scale. A personal trainer understands where you need help and focuses on your recovery through the right program.

Motivation – You don't get it when you need it

Motivation has generally been observed as one of the most frequently researched topics in the field of psychology and education. It is the energy that drives people to do something consistently and progressively. Nevertheless, due to the complexity of motivation, there are different views and understandings of the connotation of the term. Have you ever given a thought to the fact – why do we feel a lack of motivation when we need it the most?

Considering that autonomous motivation is more likely to energize you and drive long-term behaviour change than guided motivation, it is crucial to understand the factors that can contribute to your motivation. As I discussed earlier in the book, motivation is categorized into two sections – intrinsic and extrinsic. In truth, our motivation is often a mixture of both intrinsic and extrinsic factors. In fitness, people are driven by extrinsic factors first, before realizing the intrinsic part of the game.

Imagine the first time you start any form of fitness regime. You have an extrinsic motive in mind, and you want to solve that problem through exercising. The motivation that drives you towards your workout is the extrinsic reinforcement for what you do. The problem with this approach is that, sometimes, the lack of intrinsic motivation creates a dependency on extrinsic motivation, which, over a period of time, becomes monotonous. If you are not internally happy with what you are doing, you would never continue doing it. Similarly, if you are exercising only when you feel motivated, you are less likely to feel motivated at all to continue it.

> Motivation is categorized into two sections – intrinsic and extrinsic.

Fitness Habits

One day you might find yourself saying, "I don't feel motivated to go for a workout," and this can take a toll on you the next day as well if you do not pull yourself back on track quickly. Lack of motivation occurs for almost all of us at some point in time despite our best efforts, and these fluctuations are a part and parcel of our daily lives. The reason why I am discussing how motivation acts, and how intricately it is ingrained within us is to demonstrate how a personal trainer can fit into the equation and help you squeeze the intrinsic motivation out of you, so that you are driven by internal happiness and do it anyway, even when the situation is adverse.

While I talk about how motivation works, it is also pertinent to know the primary components of motivation – action, consistency and intensity. Though it gets difficult for anyone to continue their workout with the same action, consistency and intensity every single day, a personal trainer can bring in all these components to ensure you get the most by investing your time in the fitness program. This explains why it's critical to invest in personal training that eventually will trigger the cues to start your fitness behaviour, and the routine will help you form it as a habit.

Mastery requires practice, and a fitness habit requires consistency. Just like any mundane work in life, everything that we do regularly becomes monotonous and lackluster.

The Personal Trainer – An Anchor for your Fitness

This affects even the best of us. We want the spark to be intact in our life, but the more routine something becomes, the more we tend to lose interest in it. Even when I talk about following a consistent fitness routine, it brings a certain level of boredom on its way to become a routine.

The more routine our actions become, the more predictable the outcomes get. We stop getting as excited as before since we do not feel any spark in the actions; there are no surprises awaiting us as an outcome and hence, the reward becomes monotonous. Beginners stop seeing any progress from their workout because the initial excitement disappears within a few weeks, before fitness becomes a habit and the workout becomes a mundane affair. We run backward and forwards looking for something exciting, something new, to keep things interesting and for something to look forward to. The fact is, often, the failure in keeping up with our fitness habit is the absence of excitement. The moment we see a dip in excitement, we look for a new form of fitness, jump into following a new diet plan, and, on the way, we slip off the wagon and dismiss the progress we had made till then.

Perhaps, this gap is best mended by a personal trainer who designs the workouts in a way that it's filled with unexpected rewards and surprises. They

> Often, the failure in keeping up with our fitness habit is the absence of excitement.

design workouts so meticulously that they are difficult enough to perplex and test our powers, yet not so difficult that we are likely to face frequent failures.

Psychologist Gilbert Brim says, "One of the important sources of human happiness is working on tasks at a suitable level of difficulty, neither too hard nor too easy." It excites us the moment we try something new. We like the challenge, especially when it seems difficult but possible. The attempt to win these challenges makes the experience interesting. This intensifies the habit-forming process and keeps up your spirit so that you come back wanting to experience something fresh yet challenging enough that induces your motivation to do better every time.

Consistency is what transforms average into excellence

Whereas knowledge and motivation are two important factors to stay committed to your fitness goal, consistency is the third powerful component that stimulates continuous engagement. Most of the time, we fail because of the lack of alignment of the two previous components – knowledge and motivation, which obstruct the third major component of the cycle – consistency. Joining a gym or starting any form of workout can keep you motivated for some time, but when the excitement of the initial phase is over, maintaining consistency becomes a hurdle to cross.

The Personal Trainer – An Anchor for your Fitness

Consistency is crucial in most areas of life – to make progress, do better work, get in shape and achieve some degree of success. It is difficult to be consistent since we prefer to focus on the end result rather than the process. During the struggle, most of us quit before we can taste the benefits of staying in the course. It is easy to slip a day or two when there is a dip in motivation – and there lies the problem. Society makes us believe the concept – go big or go home. We are seasoned to an *all or nothing* mindset. Therefore, we fail to measure the contribution of small steps, of regular and sustained efforts that make a real difference in forming a fitness habit and making progress.

We do not realize how important it is to show up even when we are not the master of the art. Our lack of consistency can be incredibly frustrating and painful. Having a trainer by your side can give you the encouragement you need to pull up your socks and show up anyway. Researchers say that we perform better when we have an accountability partner. Your personal trainer is the one who makes sure you show up every day, put in your reps and do what already works, just by maintaining consistency.

Progress often hides behind boring solutions. But nobody wants to be bored. We want the results, we like things to be exciting, we like the feeling of

> Progress often hides behind boring solutions.

accomplishment. We keep our eyes on success, but we often ignore the significance of all the preceding actions. As we fall into the vicious cycle of the all or nothing mentality, we start doubting the power of consistency. This not only curtails growth, but also delays the process of improvement, and we end up getting discouraged. This is why having an accountability partner like your personal trainer is so crucial for transformation. They will have your back and pull you up during the ugly parts of your fitness journey when you are at your lowest low and feel like giving up.

We quantify our progress with the effort we put in; we overvalue the outcome and undervalue the importance of small and consistent practice that leads us to form our fitness habit. While you put your effort into maintaining a routine, your personal trainer emphasizes on making your learning fruitful, keeps your curiosity intact and focuses on curating your training as something that you would love to follow. He encourages you to take one step at a time, sees you falter and inspires you to affix your eye on your goal while ensuring that you get better with each session.

In addition, a trainer saves you from the guilt of missing a day's progress even when you have a bad day. They let you fail yet pull you out of the pit towards improvement. They ensure that you realize that there is no good or bad workout, it's only the way to progress. While your trainer leads you through a workout routine, he or she shows you the best way to exercise and makes sure you enjoy the process just as much. It is easy to get stuck in a rut when you are seeking constant victories. Your trainer ensures that you do not remain stuck.

You must follow the course designed to focus on your specific fitness growth. They plan a structured program, keeping in mind your potential, strengths and weaknesses, which will not only help them to help you better, but will also ensure that your efforts result in visible changes. There are three major components that can help you stick to your fitness goal, along with some extra push from a personal trainer – enhancing your knowledge about fitness, keeping up your motivation level and following a consistent routine.

Above all, working out is more fun when you have a partner who looks at the same goal as you do and assists you in your progress. Your personal trainer is the one who you stay accountable to for every move you make in fitness, every class you miss, and every workout that you escape. Even after ten years of fitness training, I enjoy how my trainer pushes me to learn and improve, which in turn leads to sustainable growth.

We always like to measure how far we have come; we love to present ourselves as successful to the people around us; we strive to become our best selves. We try to look our

Fitness Habits

best when we go out or meet people, we make constant efforts to make people around us accept and praise us. The fitness habit is one such habit that makes us look like an improved version of ourselves and helps us to look like an impressive person who chooses to stay healthy. Taking care of ourselves and doing things that make us look fit and presentable have always attracted eyeballs, and fitness is the way to achieve this in a tough yet straightforward manner. This is precisely why personal training has gained so much popularity and works so well when you want to achieve a better, healthier and fitter body.

The Personal Trainer – An Anchor for your Fitness

TAKEAWAYS

- A personal trainer is an expert who understands the best exercises according to your level of fitness and applies the right strategies correctly for you.
- There are three key components that will help you keep up with your fitness target along with some additional support from a personal trainer – enhancing your fitness awareness, maintaining your motivation level and following a daily schedule.
- A personal trainer helps you bridge the gap between your current fitness status and your fitness goal.
- A personal trainer helps squeeze the intrinsic motivation out of you so that you are driven by internal happiness rather than waiting for motivation to form your fitness habit.
- A personal trainer helps you realize that 'less is more if done correctly' when compared to the general idea of 'go big or go home'.

8
Get Ready to Reset!

Congratulations if you have come this far. This means you have a strong urge to change your present lifestyle. That you have decided on taking the first step towards making fitness a habit. To take on the challenge to make fitness a habit, confront this next level, open this new chapter in your life, and press the reset button for a better and fitter tomorrow. Choosing your battle is half-way to winning, and by this, I mean when you choose to put your step forward for what you desire, you shift your decision from remaining the same to making the effort to change. And the pillar of your decision is – finding your why and knowing what matters the most.

This chapter will give you an insight on how to take forward your fitness journey, or rather just start from whatever fitness level you are at. I will also sum up the key areas that you should engrave into your mind and aim towards enabling competence, so that it helps you in building your fitness habits gradually. This chapter focuses on what we have covered in this book so far, which will direct you towards making fitness a habit.

Find your *why*

Discovering your *why* not only guides you through every step you take, but also helps you progress with a clear vision. Similarly, your *why* in fitness gives your fitness a purpose that leads you to take the steps towards *how* to set your fitness habit and follow through.

Finding your *why* will ensure your commitment to fitness. When the reasons (*why*) behind your intention to change is vague, it is easier to get caught up in excuses and never being able to bring yourself to the point of doing specific things to get positive results. Without craving, there is no action (*routine*), and the craving lies in defining your *why*.

The greater the craving, the stronger the habit.

Start small

Habits like fitness establish a sense of self-improvement and it's an investment that will reap major benefits in the future for your health, both mentally and physically. Any change looks

> Finding your why will ensure your commitment to fitness.

uncomfortable in the beginning. Working out is no different. Anything new looks tough in the beginning and that is why it requires a result-oriented strategy.

Any change or modification in your regular lifestyle doesn't come naturally. Whether you want to lose the extra kilos or want a fitter body, a change that focuses on reaching smaller fitness goals can work as a huge motivating factor as this gives you a sense of accomplishment.

Start as small as you can – maybe walking a kilometre a day, going for a jog for ten minutes, anything that you can do without even putting much effort. And once you can do the minimum work without even thinking about it as a task, it falls into your routine. You feel more confident about your progress and that works as a motivational perk. You are exercising to challenge your body and get fitter by raising your capacity. It will get better with time, and every time you will have to pull yourself out of your comfort zone.

It is never going to be easy, but starting small and gradually building up momentum will help you sustain the journey.

Define your cue and routine

To master your fitness habits, start by fixing the first important thing – the cue. Once you have fixed the cue, it becomes easier to follow the same cue that leads you to the routine. The more obvious your cue is, the lesser are the chances of missing out on your routine. Choose a time or place or preceding action to define your cue.

Tying your fitness habit with a particular time and place helps you make your habit obvious. Pick a time when you are least cluttered with other commitments. For example, if you are an early riser and you can find time to go for a morning walk just after brushing your teeth or finishing your morning tea, follow that cue (just after finishing your morning tea) regularly to start your morning walk routine.

Similarly, it could be right after breakfast, right after you get up from the bed and freshen up, or it could be when you get home from work. Define your cue, be consistent, and let that be a reminder for you to start your routine, every single day. Once your cue is defined, it gets easier to follow through with the routine.

Attach your routine with a *reward*

Connecting your workout with a reward motivates you to follow the routine. Working out is tough and that's the reason why many people can't continue it for a long haul. But when you tie your workout with some kind of a reward – whether it is to lose weight, look better, improve your health or just plain feel good – you're more likely to stick to it. Or even

> Once your cue is defined, it gets easier to follow through with the routine.

better, try to make your workout something that gives you a sense of accomplishment, a feel-good factor in your life.

The reward you receive from working out determines the continuity of your routine. As a matter of fact, most people quit as the routine gets boring even when they have a defined reward. This is why it is crucial to not let your routine get stale with monotony and boredom. Get creative with your workouts. Mix up your workouts with something fun so that it becomes less of a tedious workout session and more like a challenging yet fun activity that leads you towards your goal. If you ask seasoned exercisers, you will find they are always looking for something new – trying to reach new fitness goals, make their fitness routine fun, challenge their bodies so that they don't fall into the rut and have fun while working out. The experience they go through from the change in their routine such as learning a new form of fitness, challenging their body differently, achieving different fitness results, work as added perks – a new form of reward.

Build a *craving*

Though you may have a cue, routine and reward in place for your fitness habit to develop, unless you have a *craving* for the reward, you will not find the urge to perform the fitness routine. We tend to continue what we once liked, i.e. the satisfactory reward.

The sense of craving for a reward makes us continue to return to the routine we had previously performed to get the same reward. Satisfaction from receiving a reward invokes motivational stimuli that lead us to replicate the same fitness activity and to shape a craving that is the key to forming a fitness habit. Craving is the significant driving force and the second stage in your fitness habit.

There is no urge to respond or act without a craving. It happens in the brain and allows the habit loop to begin. It is not the habit that we long for, but the change or feeling of an inner state. Similarly, you may not like the exhaustion working out can cause, but you start longing for the satisfaction you get after finishing a gruelling and sweaty workout session.

Associate your workout with an intrinsic reward, something that you like as a reward and the feeling it delivers every time you work out to make it a consistent practice. It could be the feeling of accomplishment, getting closer to the goal or just plain feeling active. Once you associate what you like after you finish a workout, you crave the feeling and that becomes the driving force to make fitness a lifestyle choice.

Make your workout look easy

While the reward plays an important role in making fitness a habit, making

> Associate your workout with an intrinsic reward.

your workout look easy to continue, fun or meaningful to you is another thing that keeps you going. If you are a beginner, a full-fledged HIIT workout might scare you off. Rather trying something fun and sustainable to perform will make your body and mind want to continue doing it day after day.

The key to an effective workout is to know your current limits, put enough repetitions and refinement to strengthen your competence level, and then expand your limits further. Design your workouts at a smaller level, get to know your capabilities and then step up to the next level. This way, there is less chance of you going out of control sacrificing precision and failing on your face.

Plan your workout

Planning before you do anything significantly increases the chances of actually completing it. Similarly, having a plan before starting a workout acts as a cue, helping you follow your fitness routine. Our brain is a planning mechanism and when you know what to do and for how long, your brain prompts you to follow the routine.

There may be days you wish to go for a five-kilometre run, but there are days when you struggle to do a half-an-hour workout. Listen to your body and go for a small walk or simple

> Planning your exercise works as a cue to your fitness routine.

stretching or something very minimal that will make your move but will not suck your energy out. The hope that you will be performing your routine the way you plan serves as a reminder and increases the chances of your actually doing it.

Planning your exercise works as a cue to your fitness routine. If we consider motivation as a stimulating factor in performing the exercise behaviour, the cue of planning acts as a bridge that helps you actually perform your exercise.

Stay consistent

The trick to stick to a workout routine is to do as little as you can to make it a consistent affair. Simply following the fitness routine and repeating it, even for a minimum amount of time, helps your brain form your fitness habit. Consistency is crucial in forming any habit like fitness, even when it means going slow. When you are in the stage of making workout a daily lifestyle habit, do it continuously for ninety days. On days when you don't feel like working out, keep it as minimal as 5 to10 minutes – keep it as simple as a few stretching or a 10 minute stroll. This way you are not breaking your consistency.

The progress achieved is proportional to the consistency maintained. Progress often lies in getting used to the boring process of practicing consistently, sticking to the cue and following your fitness routine. Fitness habits are a form of goal-directed automatic behaviour and consistency in fitness is a ritualistic practice that shapes your fitness habit.

Set realistic goals

The human brain loves to take up challenges that are exciting, demanding, filled with achievements and minimal occasional failures. We enjoy tasks that are challenging enough to test our strengths, but not so challenging that we are likely to face serious failure and constant troubles. Setting a realistic goal for your fitness where you define how far you can go in how long is what decides your success.

Planning your goals and expecting the temporary falls along the way is a realistic approach towards achieving anything you set your mind on. Sometimes the progress can be slow, it may feel exhausting, you may stumble along the way, you may be temporarily derailed – but it's all a part of the journey. The difference between failure and success is how fast you pick yourself up from the fall and keep going instead of quitting.

Imagine you have a goal of losing 15 kilos weight. It may seem unrealistic if you see from where you stand right now if you don't know where to start from, which exercises to do, how to do them, for how long and at what intensity. You need a plan, a workout schedule to move forward every day, every week, and months to reach the goal you are aspiring to achieve.

Get Ready to Reset!

Be analytical about what is working for you and what isn't, because if you are setting yourself up with goals that are too big to achieve, you are planning for a fall and this might make you feel like a failure. Pushing your limit is a powerful metric to step up your fitness game, but knowing how far you should push your limits ensures knowing your boundaries and progressing towards a realistic goal. Remember, if you *lay a brick every day, soon you'll have a wall.*

Your environment is your motivator

Our environment is like a magnet; it shapes our behaviour and helps us build better habits, moulds our emotions, belief system, attitude, our inspiration, the standards and expectations we set for ourselves. What we mean by the environment is the people we are surrounded with, the kind of habits they follow, their behavioural pattern – all of this makes an impact on the way we develop our habits.

It is unlikely to find someone who isn't influenced by anyone in his whole life. For example, merely working out with friends makes us workout as regularly and put in the reps, even when it gets harder. Or running with our friends makes us run faster. We tend to learn things faster when we have a

> The difference between failure and success is how fast you pick yourself up from the fall and keep going.

community that shares similar interests as we do. Having a support group in our close setup has an extremely powerful effect when they share similar goals and vibes.

Sometimes having the back of others seems to be motivating whereas in the same situation, if we are placed alone, we might lack motivation and act differently. The wisdom of crowds, of course, is often a much-celebrated phenomenon.

While we like to adopt the behaviours of others, habits like fitness can be an interesting example to show how we try to perform similar to the person we like, or how we try to outperform them sometimes. When we work out with our friends, we want to be treated as equal and do not want to look inferior. As a general rule, having someone else to equate ourselves with matters a lot, and this, as a matter of fact, makes it easier to develop habits like fitness. We want to match pace, never want to lag behind.

Track your progress

When your reward is approaching, stopping is not a choice. The principle of measuring your fitness progress is to minimize the number of slips and increase the number of small successes. It fuels the desire to keep your exercise routine regular – from beginning with a tiny jog, home workouts or spending thirty minutes on any workout at the gym. Many, including elite athletes, trust this method because monitoring changes is one of the most successful ways to prevent yourself from being demotivated. It stands as proof of your hard work and consistency.

It serves as a mechanism to make your fitness habits more addictive. When you feel low or the conditions are adverse, it is easy to slip off the track. But assessing your progress is a gentle reminder to hark back quickly so that you do not lose it all.

When you start to train, it's like turning on the power mode. Something new starts happening in your body and it goes through subtle changes, slowly moves into the active zone which your body wasn't aware of. But after a few workouts, a few days, a few weeks or a few months, your body starts to realize how to stabilize that and process into the system as a new addition to your lifestyle.

In the early phases of establishing your fitness routines, there is still a big blob of discontentment. You expect a rapid change in your body. And during the initial phase, it's shocking how pointless and minuscule the changes may appear, making you feel your efforts are inefficacious. You fail to fathom whether you are even making progress or stuck, it feels disheartening.

Keeping a track of your progress – from how much you can lift from the previous week/month, how many reps you can do without gasping for breath, to how long you can go on with a workout without giving up – your progress chart makes you realize how far you have come.

Nothing goes in vain; nothing gets wasted. Even your small attempts make a difference.

Conquer, don't compare

We are constantly comparing ourselves without considering our progress. We often lose the perception of ourselves, our struggles, our achievements and progress. We feel so dissatisfied, unworthy and futile that we repeatedly find ourselves gyrating in the vicious cycle of comparison. We are chasing the game of perfection, swept away by the clamour of the crowd. It is difficult to consider your journey as meaningful when we are surrounded by the glamour of standardized success – from luminous career choices to extravagant materialistic acquisitions. And this creates a dilemma when your efforts start looking much lesser than others, your progress seems trivial compared to others, your achievements appear inconsequential compared to the rest. Comparing yourself to others creates an illusion that you are inferior to others while it's a false belief we allow to grow within us. It makes you look inferior instead of recognizing the beauty and value of your own uniqueness.

> Your progress chart makes you realize how far you have come.

Get Ready to Reset!

Go ahead if you want to admire others on their fitness achievements, their progress and their hard work, but don't bog yourself down comparing your efforts with them. Rather, get inspired and do better. Get motivated to reach their level, learn things that brought them to that fitness level and try to improve as you move ahead.

Fitness takes time to show aesthetic outcomes but valuing only the aesthetics will not take you far. The journey towards making fitness a conscious lifestyle choice takes you through a lot of changes from improving your mood to making mindful food choices, better sleep quality, improved lifestyle habits, better time management, better productivity level and so on. These don't happen overnight. Your journey becomes more meaningful when you constantly put your step forward, come what may.

You may ask, "If I don't compare my body with someone else's, who do I compare myself to?"

The answer is – the past YOU!

Take a step from wherever you stand and stay consistent to improve every time you go for a workout. That's when you grow, you shed your old skin and become a better version of yourself, you become the conqueror.

There is no one way to succeed. There will always

> Your journey becomes more meaningful when you constantly put your step forward, come what may.

be someone else who will be doing better than you. The only way to reach your fitness goal is to follow the path you have chosen for yourself because when you choose something for yourself, you put your faith and effort into bringing the best out of it. You shine.

Every effort matters when you choose fitness as a lifestyle. You progress every day when you choose to go ahead with your workout, even if for ten minutes. Your small efforts with consistency weave your progress together and you succeed in the way you always wanted to. Developing fitness habits is just the beginning of bringing immense goodness into your life. It instigates many small habits that cumulatively lead you to the fitness results you desire. There is no good or bad workout. No workout should ever feel or look like a chore or a punishment.

Staying fit is a reward that you are bestowing on your body. Enjoy every little progress as a step to success and build your fitness habit stronger with every move.